AJAIYI AND HIS INHERITED POVERTY

Amos Tutuola was born in Abeokuta, Nigeria, in 1920. The son of a cocoa farmer, he attended several schools before training as a blacksmith. He later worked as a civil servant. His first novel, *The Palm-Wine Drinkard*, was published in 1952 and brought him international recognition. From 1956 until retirement, he worked for the Nigerian Broadcasting Company while continuing to write. His last book, *The Village Witch Doctor and Other Stories*, was published in 1990. He died in Ibadan in 1997.

by the same author

Ajaiyi and His Inherited Poverty

AMOS TUTUOLA

FABER & FABER

This edition first published in 2015
by Faber & Faber Ltd
Bloomsbury House
74–77 Great Russell Street
London WC1B 3DA

Typeset by Faber & Faber Limited
Printed in England by CPI Group (UK) Ltd, Croydon, CR0 4YY

A CIP record for this book is available from the British Library

ISBN 978–0–571–31687–8

FSC
www.fsc.org
MIX
Paper from
responsible sources
FSC® C013604

2 4 6 8 10 9 7 5 3 1

In memory of my mother
Mrs. Esther Aina Tutuola
who died on
25th November 1964

CONTENTS

9

I, as AJAIYI by name, was fifteen years of age, my junior sister, AINA by name, was twelve. Both of us were born by the same father and mother, in a very small village. This village contained only about one thousand houses. The walls of these houses were mud and the roofs were thatched with the broad leaves and spear-grasses. The whole of the inhabitants of the village were not more than four thousand.

This story happened about two hundred years ago when I first came to this world through another father and mother. By that time I was a boy and not a girl, by that time I was the poorest farmer and not as a story-teller, by that time I was the most wicked gentile and the strongest worshipper of all kinds of the false gods and not a christian, by that time I was the poorest among the people of my village and not the richest, by that time there were no cars on the roads or the aeroplanes on the sky but to trek from village to village and to cross large rivers by hand-made canoes and not by steam-ships.

By that time the father who born me got a very big hunch on his back and it was so for my mother who born me by that time. Having seen these their hunchbacks, the rest people in the village gave them the nickname "The hunchback family". They used to call us with this nickname. My father was a farmer. He worked more than the rest farmers in the village, yet he was the poorest man in the village. Because as he was working hard in his farms it was so his poverty was becoming worse. My mother was also a hard working woman, she was more industrious than the rest women in the village but she was the poorest woman in the village. Although my father and mother were the poorest in the village but they were very kind to our neighbours, strangers, animals, etc.

I was helping my father in the farm while my junior sister, Aina, was helping our mother to carry loads from the farm to the village and she was also helping her to do all the houseworks. "Remember The Day After To-morrow, my son and daughter!" That was how our father used to warn us whenever Aina and I offended one who was older than us. Sometimes, whenever we did some evil thing that which the people disliked, my father would not hesitate to warn us again: "My son and daughter, remember the day after tomorrow because it will come back to you soon or later after my death!" Alas! Aina and I were too young this time to understand this our father's warning and we were so very stupid to ask for the meaning of it from our father.

But after many years hard work, our father and mother became old and weary. So old and weary that both of them could not work any more for our living. Having seen this, I, as their only merciful son, started to work alone in my father's farms as little as I could. Although I was still young yet I could get little yams, etc., from the farms to feed my old father, mother, my junior sister, Aina and myself.

One afternoon, my father and mother sat closely on very old native chairs. Each of these chairs was partly worn out and nearly eaten off by the ants. Rags and old baskets were hung on every part of the sitting room, while refuses, old basins, plates, etc., were scattered on the floor. But as Aina and I sat on the mud pavement in the front of the house and we were singing loudly with cheerful voices to the hearing of our mother and father as both of them were thinking seriously about their poverty. As Aina and I were still singing loudly with cheerful voices, my father spoke to my mother with a sorrowful voice that —"I am very sorry, we are going to die soon!" Then my mother interrupted hastily with the same sorrowful voice that—"And we are going to leave our only son and daughter in our this poverty!"

Of course, Aina and I did not hear these sorrowful discussions at all. But we were still singing loudly with melodious voices and laughter to the hearing of our mother and father that—"How poor we are! How poor we are! How poor we are!" etc. After a few minutes that we had been singing this song, both of us stood up and we continued to sing this song loudly as we were entering the sitting room in which our mother and father sat. When we met both of them as they dropped down their heads which showed us that they were thinking about our poverty with sorrow that moment. Then Aina and I stopped singing at the same time. So as both of us stood before them, and then they lifted up their heads and were looking at us. I asked from my father loudly:—"Father! Are we going to die in this our poverty? But of course, I believe, you have inherited it from your fore-father!" As Aina and our mother were still looking on, my father replied with grief: "Of course my fore-father might have died in poverty, and as well as I am going to die in poverty soon. But now, I will make it clear to you that if father and mother die in poverty, it does not mean that their children will die in poverty as well if they can work hard."

Then I asked again from my father with a clear voice: "But father, I wonder, you are working more and you get more farms and crops than the other farmers in this village! You know, my father, this village contains about four thousand people, but we are the poorest among them all!" Then my father shook his head up and down and he replied with sorrow: "Well, of course, maybe all the other farmers in this village are not poor. But I believe one thing, that you or your own sons may be free from this our poverty provided you or your own sons continue to work hard."

But as I wanted to know from my father how this our poverty had started. I asked from him again: "But you told me now, my father, that if I continued to work hard we might be free from this our poverty. But my father, I notice one thing that the more we are working hard in the farm the more our poverty is becoming worse. Why is that so, my father?" Again, my father hastily explained that: "Well, maybe as we are working very hard in the farm it is so our poverty is growing up like a tree. You should not be discouraged by that. But I will advise you now that you should continue to work hard, and . . !" But as my father wanted to continue his explanations about the poverty, Aina interrupted suddenly with a loud voice as she faced our mother. She said—"But I do not agree to our father's explanations that we should continue to work hard. Because I notice that you, as our mother, is very industrious and you work more than any of the women who are in this village. But as you are growing old it is so our poverty is growing worse along with you! Why is that so, my mother?"

Then our mother breathed in and out heavily and she replied sorrowfully that—"Although I am very industrious and I am still in poverty, that does not mean that I

am destined with poverty. Anything can happen to a
person who is born under this sun. But I advise you now
that you and Ajaiyi should not be discouraged by our
continuous poverty. We are not destined with poverty at
all as the rest people in the village had thought us to be!"
Our mother hardly explained to Aina like that when a
middle aged man who was a joker began to knock at the
door heavily. He knocked at the door so heavily that it
broke into two and it hardly fell down to the left part of the
sitting room, when he (Joker) entered unexpectedly without looking at the broken door. Immediately the Joker
entered, he stood in the middle of the sitting room and
began to look at the refuses, rags, old plates, basins, etc.
Then he shouted funnily—"Hah! although you are not
wealthy in money but you are really wealthy in rags and
refuses! Is it n't?" the Joker asked and looked at all of us
funnily.

At the same time, my father replied with a cheerful
voice—"Of course you are right, Joker! But you too are
wealthy in joking which probably you have inherited from
your fore-father and .. !" But as my father was still telling
him like that he interrupted suddenly with great laughter
—"Of course, a sheep never change its skin until it dies!
So I believe, you too will not be free from your poverty
until you will die! Will you?" the Joker asked funnily
from my father. But when Joker said that we would not
be free from our poverty until we would die, my father,
mother, Aina and I, scattered suddenly to every part
of the sitting room and we were scrambling sticks. Then
all of us chased this Joker out of our house with the sticks
as we were shouting on him greatly: "Hah, you hopeless
Joker, cursed us that we would not be free from our

poverty! Go out! Go out! You hopeless Joker!" Then we chased him far away before we came back to the sitting room.

But we hardly came back to the sitting room when my mother became ill suddenly. She became so seriously ill that Aina and I hastily laid her on the mat in the sitting room. Then both of us, my father and four of our neighbours sat round her and we began to take care of her as quickly as we could. After a few minutes she became a very little conscious. After a while she began to talk but with a very faint voice. It was very hardly to understand all the words that which was speaking out this time. But when she wanted to stop the last breath, then she began to advise Aina and I as she was dying—"Now I am dying and I am leaving both of you in our poverty but do not be discouraged to continue to work hard. You will be all right in the near future if you . . . work . . . hard." Then she died.

Immediately she was dead Aina and I started to weep loudly and we were staggering about in the house as our neighbours and my father took our dead mother to the backyard and then they buried her there. After she was buried, my father staggered back to the sitting room as our four neighbours went back to their houses. Having seen how Aina and I were weeping repeatedly, my father began to caress us just to comfort us. He caressed us for a few minutes before he began to talk to us: "Do not think so much about your mother. Because she has left this our poverty for riches in heaven. She is now in heaven and in riches!" But when my father told us that our dead mother had gone to the riches in heaven and that she was no more in poverty, Aina and I exclaimed with happiness at a time:

"Is that so? Our mother is now in riches in heaven! Very well!"

Aina and I were very happy when my father comforted us like that. We wiped away the tears from our cheeks at the same time. But after our neighbours who came to sympathize with us went back to their houses, I pointed finger to my father's hunch and asked from him: "My father, I suggest that it is this your big hunch that which makes us poor like this!" But my father lifted his head up and replied at the same time: "Not at all! A hunch does not make a person poor!" My father hardly replied like that when Aina interrupted with a loud sharp voice— "But father, all the people who have no humps on their backs are always rich! There is none of them who is in poverty like us! I wonder!" When my junior sister, Aina, interrupted like that and before my father replied I supported her hastily that—"Oh, yes! You are right, Aina! I have been thinking of the same thing as well that all the people who have no hunch on their backs are not in poverty like us!" As I supported Aina like that then my father replied that—"My children, don't deceive your-selves. A hunch does not hinder the progress of the person who has it on his back!" Then I replied with a doubtful mind that—"But of course, you may be right, my father!" At this stage, Aina had no interest in these arguments again. But she said suddenly: "Anyhow, let us stop the arguments about the hunch first. But what are we going to eat as dinner now because I am badly hungry for food and the night is coming nearer?" Of course when Aina said that she was hungry for food, we discontinued the arguments at the same time.

But it was a great pain to me as I could not find out and

know what had caused my father's poverty from beginning so that I might know how to achieve it. But as I was also badly hungry for food this time I supported Aina that I was hungry for food. When my father heard from us that we were hungry, he asked: "Is there anything in the house to eat this night?" So, at the same time, Aina and I stood up, we walked to the pots which were in the sitting room but all were empty except a big pot which was in a corner was full of cold water.

When we found that there was nothing in the house to eat, we told my father that—"There is no even a single crumb of food in all of the pots!" After a while, my father asked as he pointed a hand to the pot of water—"Hope there is water in that pot?" So as I was looking on anxiously to eat, Aina replied: "Yes, the pot is full up with the cold water!" Then my father shouted with a smile: "That's O'kay, my children! We have something to take this night then!" But without hesitation, I asked: "Are we going to drink water instead of food this night?" And my father replied at the same time that: "Yes! That's what we have!" But as we heard like that from my father, Aina and I shouted—"Father, you are really destined with poverty then!"

At last, when we found nothing in the house to eat except the cold water. We poured plenty of the water in a big bowl and brought it before my father. Both of us sat in front of him and then all of us drank it with a small calabash. After we drank the water which was meant a dinner for us, then the light was quenched, we laid down on the mats and we slept.

THE FUNERAL CEREMONY OF MY
FATHER AND MOTHER

In the morning, Aina and I woke up and we dressed up in the little rags which we got. Then we went near my father who still lay on the mat. But we were very sad when we met him seriously ill. We greeted him with the voice of morning greetings as both of us were greeting him every morning. But my father could hardly reply with very faint sick voice. When both of us saw that he was seriously ill, we helped him to sit up on the mat but he became so feeble suddenly this time that he was unable to sit up without supporting him with hands or other thing. So we leaned him against the wall. As he began to shake from feet to head, we gave him a kind of medicine to take but he could not open his mouth to swallow it. Having failed in all of our efforts to bring him back to normal with the medicine then we began to look at him.

After a while, he spoke to us but with a very faint sick voice. He waved hand to us to kneel down before him to pray for us. So both of us knelt down before him with great respect. But as we knelt down before my father, a kidnapper of children came to the window. He peeped in through the window and he was listening to my father's prayers but we were not aware that a kidnapper was peeping in through the window.

Then my father prayed for both of us: "As both of you

19

had helped me to live to this moment, it is so your own sons and daughters will do for you. You will not die in poverty as I am going to die in poverty soon. But further-more, I shall not forget to advise you again that you must not forget 'Remember The Day After Tomorrow.' But you must put in your minds always that 'Remember The Day After Tomorrow' shall come back to you soon after death. You, my children, you must keep yourselves away from the kidnappers. You must not go too far away from this village after my death so that you may not be kid-napped, because you are still too young to defend your-selves from the bad people. But I remind you once more that you should remember—'Remember The Day After Tomorrow' who will come back to you soon. After my death and when I reach the heaven, your mother and I shall be looking after you from the heaven. Goodbye, my dear son and daughter. Goodbye, goodbye, goodbye to y-o-u." So after the prayers, my father began to fall down slowly as his sick voice began to fade away as he was waving his right hand to us with sorrow. Then he fell down and stopped breath at the same time.

As soon as my father fell down and died, the kidnapper who peeped in through the window and had heard how my father had warned us that we must remember "Remember The Day After Tomorrow" before he died, talked to himself as he was leaving the window for the place of his abode that: "Yes, I have heard how their father had warned them before he died. He warned them that they should remember 'Remember The Day After Tomorrow.' I have a very good chance now to convince Aina and Ajaiyi. I will tell them that I am the very 'Remember The Day After Tomorrow.' And I will tell them also that I am their eldest brother!" It was like that this kidnapper thought within himself to deceive us before he went away.

My father hardly fell down and died when Aina and I became unhappy unexpectedly. We were so perplexed that we did not know when we ran to our nearby neighbours. We told them that my father had died a few minutes ago. Without hesitation, our neighbours followed us back to the house and they were equally unhappy when they saw that he had died as we told them. When they were quite sure that my father had died. The first two things that which they first asked from us were the new white cloth and the coffin with which to bury him.

"Have you got ready the new white cloth and the coffin for your father?" all of them shouted together with voice of levity. But as our neighbours asked us these two things, Aina and I were greatly ashamed, because we were so poor that we got no money to buy the white cloth and the coffin which were essential for a dead person. And as it was our custom that every dead person must be buried with white cloth and coffin or if the family of the deceased could not afford or was too poor to buy these two things for their deceased, their neighbours and the other people in the village would be making a mockery of them throughout their lives time and that they would recognise even a goat more than them. So without hesitation, I told our neighbours with tears that the white cloth and the coffin would be ready in a few hours time. Having promised them like that they told us that they would return to their houses first but they would return as soon as the white cloth and the coffin were ready. Then they went back to their houses.

As soon as our neighbours went back to their houses,

Aina and I sat down in front of our dead father. We began to think how we could get money to buy the white cloth and the coffin. After a while, it came to my mind that there was a good woodcarver who lived in the next village. This village was at a distance of about four miles from our own village.

Without hesitation, I stood up, I told Aina that I was going to see that woodcarver to beg him to carve a coffin for our dead father. Then without money in hand, I went to the woodcarver. I told him that I wanted him to carve a coffin for me from a very good wood and that the coffin should have attractive ornaments. I explained to him furthermore that I would wait until he would complete it so that I might carry it to my village at the same time.

"If you want a very fine coffin with various kinds of attractive ornaments on it, you will pay two pounds for it!" the woodcarver told me the cost of a fine coffin. When he asked me to pay two pounds for the coffin, I explained to him with tears that I got no even a half-penny in hand or at home. When he heard so from me, he first refused to carve it. But when I begged him for a few minutes and promised with tears that after a few days that my father had been buried, then I would come back to him to do any kind of work which he might give me to do for him to cover the cost of the coffin.

Having explained to this woodcarver like that, he asked me to tell him the name of my father. When I told him his name, he shouted that he knew my father. He said although he was poor but he was very kind to almost every person before he died. When he said so, he stood up and as he was taking all his carving instruments, he told me with a cheerful voice that he would carve a nice coffin

22

for me with free of charge because my father was kind throughout his life time. When he took all his carving instruments, he told me to follow him and I did so. We went to the back of his house where there was a good wood which he had already carved into a fine coffin with various ornaments on it but it remained only the last touches for him to complete it.

Then without hesitation, he started to do the last touches and when he worked hard, he finished the last touches within one hour. Then he and with the help of another man, they put it on my head and then I started to carry this beautiful coffin to my village. But I was not so happy as I was carrying it along the road to my village because I never knew yet where to get money to buy the white cloth although I had got a fine coffin for free of charge for my father in respect of his kindness when he was alive. However, when I trekked as fast as I could, I reached the village at about nine o'clock in the night.

But as I was carrying this coffin along in the village to the house, some of the people of the village who thought that we were so poor that we would not be able to buy a coffin with which to bury my father were ashamed. But it was so many of the people of the village who liked my father, ran to me, they took the coffin from my head with happiness, they put it on their shoulders. Then all of them began to sing the funeral dirge and all of us were dancing along to the house. When we came to the house, they entered with me and they put the coffin down in front of my dead father who was still in the sitting room since when he had died. Having put the coffin down gently, they returned to their houses as they were still singing cheerfully.

23

But as I struggled very hard before I could get the coffin and brought it to the house. I met another sorrow in the house as well which was darkness. Every part of the house was so dark that one could not even see himself at all. Then at the same time, I shouted: "Aina! Aina! Aina! Where are you?" But there was no answer and there was no trace of her. Within this moment, I could not say, whether Aina had run to hide in another village for shame because she thought we could not get the white cloth and coffin to bury our father. Again, to add more to my sorrow, the whole people who helped me to carry the coffin to the house had gone back to their houses without staying with me as long as necessary when they saw that there was no light in the house but the darkness. As soon the people had left, I left the sitting room just to go to the front of the house to think how to get money like a half-penny to buy the palm-oil to be used for the lamps. As I left the sitting room to the verandah, just a few steps to get to the outside, I stumbled on one of my father's old stools and I fell down and my head knocked the floor so heavily that it started to bleed out at the same time.

However, with great pain and the blood which was gushing out to every part of my body, I went to the outside. I stood and I began to think three things in mind at a time. Firstly, I was thinking how to get the palm-oil to be used for the lamps, secondly, I was thinking where to get Aina and thirdly, I was thinking how to get the money to buy the white cloth with which to bury my father. But God was so good, as I was still thinking all these three things in mind at a time, an old woman who was a close friend to my father, came this time with the hope to stay with me and sympathize with me for a few minutes. When she came and met me at the front of the house, she stopped, she greeted me and I answered with a dead voice.

But when she noticed that there was no light in the house, she asked: "Why do you not put light in the house and in the front of the house as well?" I explained to her at the same time that I got no money to buy the palm-oil. To my surprise, I hardly explained to her like that when this old woman went back to her house. A few minutes later, she came back with four native lamps and one pot of palm-oil. Then both of us entered the house, but as she was helping me to light up the lamps in the house, Aina came with the white cloth. Not knowing that she too left for another village to get the cloth immediately I left the village to get the coffin. As soon as she reached that village, she asked for the cloth-seller from a small girl that she first met.

Without hesitation, the girl took her to the house of the only cloth-seller who lived in this village. Because this village was so small that there was only one old woman who was selling clothes there. So when Aina explained to the cloth-seller that her father had just died, but as there was no white cloth with which to bury him, she therefore came to her to buy one piece of the white cloth in credit. Furthermore, Aina explained to her that after the funeral ceremony had been performed, then she would come back to her to do any kind of work that which she might give her to do for her to cover the cost of the cloth.

Having explained to this cloth-seller like, Aina began to weep. Having seen how she was weeping, this old woman who was the cloth-seller, shook her head up and down sadly. Then she explained to Aina that: "Your father was well known to me and I was well known to him as well as the money is well known to every person! Although he was in great poverty throughout his life time, but he was very kind to every person throughout his life time. Now, for your father's kindness when he was alive, take this piece of the white cloth for free of charge. But do not come back to me with the hope to do work for the cost of the cloth!" So with gladness Aina knelt down, she took the white cloth from this old woman. Having thanked her greatly, Aina returned to our village. Although as there was darkness on the road it was very difficult for her to trek as quickly as she wanted to, but however, she reached the village at about ten o'clock in the night.

I was extremely happy when Aina brought this white cloth to the house. It was like that we got the white cloth for free of charge as well as the coffin. But as soon as I took it from her it came to my mind this moment that we got no money which was to be paid for the tailor who would sew it. Of course, when I thought over and over where to get the money and I did not know. Aina advised me to take it to one tailor who lived at the extreme end of the village. She said that perhaps he would sew it for us in credit.

When Aina advised me like that, I was ashamed to go to the tailor and tell him to sew the cloth for me in credit. But it came to my mind that we could not wear it for our father without sewing it. Then I sold my shame away and I went to the tailor at the same time. When I gave the cloth to him I told him to sew it for me but in credit. But I would come back to him to do the work which would cover the cost of his workmanship. But it was a great surprise to me that the tailor bursted

26

into a great laughter instead to tell me how much I would pay for his workmanship.

Having laughed for a few minutes, he said with smiling face: "Your father was kind to me and to other people when he was alive. Therefore, I am not going to take anything from you as my workmanship, but I shall sew the cloth for free of charge. Although your father was in poverty throughout his life time but he was kind!" When he said so, he began to sew this cloth. But of course it took him some hours before he finished it because he sew it with hand. So he hardly finished it when I took it from him and I thanked him greatly before I ran with it to the house. But I reached the house at four o'clock in the morning.

Having brought the cloth to the house, the old men who came to sympathize with us all the while, took the cloth from me and they wore it for my father at the same time. Now my father was beautifully laid in the sitting room and the people came to pay him their last visits till four o'clock in the evening. By four o'clock prompt, he was put in the coffin. As soon as the coffin was nailed up the people helped us to carry it. All of us were singing the funeral dirge loudly until they carried him to the outskirt of the town where he was buried. The place where he was buried was about one mile distance from the town. Having buried him there then the whole of us sang back to the village. The people accompanied us to the house before they went back to their houses. It was like that my father and mother died in poverty.

27

I PAWNED MYSELF FOR MONEY

~~~~~~

Now, it remained Aina and myself in the house. We were not happy at all because we were no more with our mother and father, both of them had died and left us in the poverty.

In the following morning, some of our neighbours advised me to go and pawn myself for money that which we would spend for the funeral ceremony of our father which would take place in a few days time. Having thanked the neighbours for their advice, Aina and I left the village for another village where a woman pawn-broker lived. When we entered her house, we met her in a well decorated sitting room. Then we knelt down before her and greeted her—"Good morning, the pawn-broker!"

"Yes, what do you want?" the pawnbroker lifted her head up and asked with a huge voice. As Aina was looking on, I told the pawnbroker—"well, I come to pawn myself for money!"

"You little boy like this! But what are you going to do with the money?" the pawnbroker asked with wonder.

"I am going to spend the money for the funeral cere-mony of my father who died recently!" I replied to the pawnbroker loudly.

"But I think you are still too young to do hard work," the pawnbroker said with pride.

"Although I am still young but I am very strong

enough to do hard work. You know, I was born and bred in poverty!" I explained without shame.

"All right, come nearer and let me test your body to know whether you are strong enough to do hard work!" the pawnbroker pressed every part of my body with both hands for about thirty minutes with doubtful mind.

"Ajaiyi is very strong to do hard work, madam!" Aina told the pawnbroker with a sharp voice.

"Well, of course, I shall give you only two pounds but you will be working for me from morning till two o'clock everyday and I am not going to feed you. Take the two pounds but you must come to start work as soon as you have finished the funeral ceremony of your father. But put it in your mind that you will be working for me until you will be able to refund my two pounds!" the pawnbroker reluctantly gave me only two pounds.

However, I took the money from the pawnbroker. Then Aina and I thanked her greatly as we were leaving. So we came back to the village. The following day, we cooked many kinds of food and bought all kinds of drinks. Then all of my father's friends, neighbours, drummers and singers were invited. All of them ate to their satisfaction. After that the drummers started to beat their drums and as all of us were singing the song of funeral and dancing, it was so everyone was drinking the drinks. So when it was daybreak the people, Aina and I danced round the village before the people went back to their houses. It was like that we performed the funeral ceremony of my father in respect of which I pawned myself for two pounds.

Now, my father's warning before he died that we should remember "The Day After Tomorrow" came to the truth because almost everything which we used for his burial and funeral ceremony were given to us for free of charge in respect of his kindnesses to his neighbours and other people. But this proverb or warning was still a puzzle to us. We had not yet understood it well. However, after my father's funeral ceremony, I started to go and work for the pawnbroker from morning till two o'clock without giving me food. But for the rest part of the day, I used to go and work in my late father's farm. So I was getting yams, etc. which Aina and I were eating.

WE WERE KIDNAPPED AND SOLD

One day as Aina and I sat in our father's sitting room and we were thinking seriously about—"Remember The Day After Tomorrow" as my father used to warn us in his days whenever Aina and I offended someone or one who was older than us. Of course, it was a pity to us later on that we did not attempt to ask my father, before he died, the meaning of his warning.

As Aina and I sat in the sitting room this day and I began to suggest to her; "Perhaps, 'Remember The Day After Tomorrow' is the name of our eldest brother who was born and had left our father for another town before we were born!" I suggested to Aina like that. "And probably our father was just warning us not to forget him," Aina supported my suggestion. At last, both of us confirmed that "Remember The Day After Tomorrow" was the name of our eldest brother who had left our father for another town before we were born.

After some months that my father had died, a strange man came to my father's house. This strange man was an expert trickster and kidnapper of children. He was the very kidnapper who peeped through the window to the sitting room and he heard how my father prayed for us and then warned us not to forget "Remember The Day After Tomorrow" when he wanted to die. But as this kidnapper noticed well that my father got a big hunch on his back. So one day, he put a flat stone on his back in such a perfect way that this stone seemed exactly a hunch when he wore a big garment over it. Having done so, he came to my father's house and he met us as we sat in our father's sitting room.

"Hello sir! Welcome sir! Please have a seat sir!" Aina and I received this kidnapper with great respect especially when we saw the costly garment which he wore over his false hunchback and also the costly big horse tail which he held as if he was a chief.

"This is the cold water, sir!" I ran to the pot and brought the cold water. I knelt down before him with great respect as I was giving him the water. After he drank it and rested for a few minutes, he asked from us as if he had not yet heard of the death of my father and mother:

"By the way, where is your father?"

"Father? Our father had died a few months ago!" Aina and I replied at a time with sorrow. "Died or what?" the kidnapper asked with a deceiving voice. "Yes, he had died and left us in his poverty!" both of us explained to him loudly.

"Could you remember that your father warned you before he died that you must not forget—'Remember The Day After Tomorrow'?" the kidnapper asked and pretended as if he was in grief.

"Oh, yes, our father used to warn us always before his death that we must remember—'Remember The Day After Tomorrow', and he told us also that—'Remember The Day After Tomorrow' would come home soon after his death!" both of us exclaimed hastily.

"Was that so? Good!" the kidnapper asked and then paused for a few minutes as he began to raise his head up and down in a slow motion as if he was thinking seriously

32

about our father's death. "Now, I confess to both of you that I am your eldest brother, whose name your father, before his death, was mentioning to you always. And my name is 'Remember The Day After Tomorrow' and I am this before you today [he stood up and posed himself with pride before us for a few minutes and then he sat back]. I was born and went to another town before both of you were born. Therefore, both of you are my junior brother and sister because your father was my father as well. So I come today to stay with you and I shall be taking great care of you as well as our father did before he died. Even to believe that I am your eldest brother, the first born of our father! [the kidnapper stood up, he showed us his false hunchback and then he sat back.] Look at my hunchback."

"Yes, we believe that you are our eldest brother and your hunchback which resembles that of our father also proves that you are our eldest brother whose name is— 'Remember The Day After Tomorrow'," the kidnapper had persuaded us with his trick and we admitted at the same time that he was our eldest brother.

"By the way, where is you mother who is my mother as well?" the kidnapper asked from us loudly with trick.

"Our mother died before the death of our father!" we replied with sorrow.

"And so both of them had left you in their poverty?" the kidnapper asked as he lighted his long and curved smoking pipe.

"Yes, we have already inherited their poverty!" we replied with tears.

"Hoo—hoo—hoo!" the kidnapper, with his trick, having heard like that from us, he covered his head with both palms pretended to be weeping bitterly for some minutes. But he did all this also just to convince us that he was our eldest brother.

"Hah, stop weeping, brother! What are you doing all this for! Please stop that, sir!" both of us stood up and caressed him until he stopped.

Then he stood up. He walked to every part of the house. He peeped to every room just to see the kind of the property which were inside them.

"But I wonder, our father and mother were so poor that they did not leave any precious property for you except rags, cutlasses and hoes! Hah, I believe now that they were really created with poverty!" the kidnapper shouted as he was returning to the sitting room and then he sat back. So with gladness, Aina went to the kitchen. She cooked the little yam that we got in the house. She brought it to him and all of us ate it together.

After a few days that this kidnapper had been living with us he advised us: "I believe, things are too dull in this village. Therefore, I shall take both of you to the town where I came from. You will be working in that town and I believe, in one year's time, everyone of you will become rich and then you will be free from the poverty which you have inherited from our father and mother. Then you will come back to this village as rich persons!" The kidnapper deceived us just to be able to take us to another town and sell us as slaves.

"Thank you, brother, for your useful advice. But who will be taking care of the house when you take us away?" I asked him with surprise.

"Never mind about the house, my junior brother, and don't be afraid, there is no any valuable property in this house which can attract the thieves to carry away. Look at this juju [he showed us one wrapped leaf] which I am going to hang on the main door now. Its wonderful work is to keep all the thieves away from this house!" The kidnapper stood up, he walked to the main door and hung the wrapped leaf there.

Then by four o'clock in the following morning, before our neighbours and other people woke in the village, the kidnapper took us to another town which was far away from our village. As soon as he took us to this foreign town, he again took us to the house of a wealthy slave-buyer who was also a very strong idol worshipper of this town. When we followed him to the sitting room of this slave-buyer, we met him sat on a high chair which was made of bamboo. He wore black native garment and a big red native cap was on his head. He sat on that bamboo chair at the centre of his sitting room. Several fearful idols were on each corner of the room. The height of each of them was up to that of a tall and huge person. The fresh blood was flowing down from their heads to their feet and this showed us that this slave-buyer or idol worshipper was sacrificing living creatures or human being to them frequently.

Immediately we entered the sitting room, the kidnapper greeted the slave-buyer and then he sat on another bamboo chair which was on the right. He hardly sat down when he shouted on us to stand at a little distance in front of the slave-buyer and we did so at the same time with fear. Then without hesitation and with a sharp voice, the kidnapper told the slave-buyer: "Yes, I bring these two poor children for you to buy!" He pointed his finger to both of us as he was telling the slave-buyer like that.

"Good. But how much do you want to sell each of them?" the slave-buyer asked from him with a huge voice. Then the kidnapper told us to pose ourselves well for the slave-buyer just to be able to see every part of our bodies. When he forced us to pose ourselves well for the slave-buyer and we did so but as he gazed at us with his fearful eyes, the kidnapper told him: "I will sell each of them for twenty pounds and you will give me two big garments and caps in addition!" But when we knew that he wanted to sell us, we shouted greatly: "Hah, brother, do you want to sell us?" So without mercy, the kidnapper struck our mouths with a stick as he boomed on us: "Shut up your mouths there! Don't you know *whom* you are talking to?"

But as soon as he became hostile to us like that unexpectedly I became so annoyed that I told him: "But don't be harsh to us like this at this time! Please, remember that you have confessed to us that you were our eldest brother whose name is 'Remember The Day After Tomorrow'!" Having heard like that from me, he stood up suddenly and shouted greatly on us: "Who is your brother? Tell me now! Who is your brother?" then he sat back as the slave-buyer was still gazing at every part of our bodies. "I am afraid, everything has now been changed here," Aina whispered to me with fear.

Then the slave-buyer turned his face to him and told him: "Well, I can pay only ten pounds for each of the children because they are very young. They cannot work in the farm but of course, I shall sacrifice them to my idols in the next festival which will take place in a few weeks time!"

"You are going to sacrifice us to your idols or what do

you say?" Aina and I shouted with fear as we stared at him.

"I say shut up your mouths there! Will you pose yourselves once more to the slave-buyer!" the kidnapper shouted on us with a fearful voice. Then he turned his eyes back to the slave-buyer and said: "All right, pay the money now. But of course, each of them is worth more than ten pounds!"

Then without hesitation, this slave-buyer or idol worshipper paid him the money and he gave him two native garments and two native caps before he told him to go away. But as this kidnapper was going away, I shouted with tears: "Hah, you sold us!" and Aina shouted with tears as well: "But you have told us that you were our eldest brother! But we have just been understood that you are not our brother at all!" Without shame, the kidnapper now proudly explained to us: "I am sorry that it is too late now before you do understand that—'Remember The Day After Tomorrow' is not the name of a person but it is a warning. And it should have been better if you have asked the meaning of it from your father before he died. So there would be no a kidnapper like myself who would be able to bring you from your village and then sell you as slaves like this! Goodbye!" So the kidnapper went away with laughter as Aina and I were still standing and were shaking with fear before the slave-buyer. A few minutes later, two strong men entered the sitting room. They tied our arms together with ropes and without mercy they dragged us to the compound where there was a shrine in which there was another fearful idol. Then these two men left us before this idol and then went out.

After a few minutes these two strong men came back

to us in the shrine with strong ropes in their hands. They put my both arms to my back and then tied both tightly with the rope. After that they put Aina's both hands to her back and tied both together with the rope as well. Having done so, they laid both of us flatly in front of the fearful idol which occupied the whole of the shrine. After that both of them went out. But after they had gone out, I looked at this fearful idol and I saw that many long swords were hung round it. All were dangling here and there whenever the breeze blew. The idol itself was in height of a giant, it had the shape of that of a human being from neck to the foot but its head was that of a bull with two long horns on head. But of course, the head was bigger than that of a bull and also the two horns on its head were longer and thicker than that of a bull.

When we were sure that the slave-buyer who bought us from the kidnapper was going to sacrifice us to this idol, then we began to struggle to loose the ropes away from our arms and then to escape for our lives. But we could not loose the ropes at all. After a while, I asked from Aina that "Who will save us from this place?" But Aina replied that "There is nobody who can save us except our dead father and mother."

It was like that we were tied up in this shrine till the night without giving us anything to eat. When it was about five o'clock in the following morning, the slave-buyer or the chief idol worshipper, his family, servants and his followers began to sing loudly and all were coming to this shrine as they were dancing. As we were hearing them singing loudly, Aina said with fear—"Hah, they are coming to kill us now for this idol." But as soon as they reached the entrance of the shrine, all of them stopped, they began to flatter the idol with different voices. But as they were still doing so and the drummers were still beating the drums in such a way that the chief idol worshipper, his family, servants and his followers, began to dance round the shrine like a mad person. Then this time, I did all my best to loose the rope away from my hands and God was so good the rope was cut unexpectedly. Then without hesitation, I took one of the swords which were hung round the idol. I hastily cut off the rope which was on Aina's arms.

So I hardly cut off the rope when I put her in one of the corners of the shrine. After that I held the sword firmly and then hid myself in another corner. I was waiting for them to enter and then to fight them with the sword. After a while, all of them with the drummers rushed in to the shrine as they were still dancing and singing loudly. But as soon as all of them were kept quiet unexpectedly when they did not see us in front of the idol. I rushed against the Chief Idol Worshipper (slave-buyer) but as I was about to behead him with the sword. All of them were so feared that they run away from the shrine. And they hardly rushed out when I told Aina to follow me. Then I began to chase them along to kill with the sword which I raised above my head. But as I was still chasing them about in the town to kill, they escaped into the bush without their wish.

After a while, when I could not trace them out in the bush, I told Aina to let us go away from their town. But as we were going along in the town as fast as we could, the kidnapper who sold us to the slave-buyer or the Chief Idol Worshipper, met us. As he was dressed in a big costly garment, he stopped and he proudly told us—"I am sorry

that it is too late before you do understand that—
'Remember The Day After Tomorrow' is not the name
of a person but it is a warning or proverb. And it should
have been better if you have asked for the meaning of it
from your father before he died. So there would be no a
deceiver and kidnapper like me who would be able to
kidnap you and sell you as slaves. And it is a good practice
for a person who does not understand a word, warning,
proverbs, etc., to ask for its full meaning before it is too
late! Goodbye!" The kidnapper explained to us as hastily
as he could but as I rushed to him just to behead him with
the sword, he jumped into the bush. Then Aina and I left
that town as quickly as possible to an unknown place
because we did not know the right road on which to travel
back to our village. That was how we were saved from the
chief idol worshipper or the slave-buyer who wanted to
sacrifice us to his idol. And it was in this town Aina and I
had understood the meaning of "Remember The Day
After Tomorrow." The meaning of it was also—"One will
reap what he sows." So if we sow a bad thing we must reap
a bad thing in future.

THE SPIRIT OF FIRE

∞∞∞∞∞∞∞∞∞∞∞∞∞∞∞∞∞∞∞∞∞∞∞∞∞∞∞∞

What others do to us teaches us sense.
There is no chance for other matter in the stomach
of a hungry person.

*

Immediately we left that town, we began to run away in the forest as fast we could so that the Chief Idol Worshipper and his people might not be able to capture us. Because we believed that all of them would chase us to catch. But of course, as he had wanted to sacrifice us to his idol, this had taught us a sense not to hesitate in one place and I still held the long sword which I took from the shrine of his fearful idol. It was with this sword I drove he and his people out of their town before we were able to escape into the forest.

Having travelled in the forest till eleven o'clock in the night and when we were sure that we had been freed from the Chief Idol Worshipper and his people. Then we stopped under a big tree and we sat down just to rest. But as we had been tired and we were very hungry before reaching there. We did not know when we fell down and slept. We enjoyed this sleep so much that we did not wake till when the noises of the birds woke us at about ten o'clock in the morning.

As soon as we were woken by the terrible noises of these birds, we stood up but as there was no river or pond which was near there. We went to the nearby weeds and then we washed our faces with the little dew that which we could collect from them. Having washed our faces with the dew we came back to that tree, I took the sword from the ground and then we continued our journey in this endless forest. When we travelled for about one hour luckily we came to a mighty tree and we stopped under it. And when we looked at it very well we saw that it was a dika-nut tree or wild mango tree with uncountable ripen fruits on its branches.

But as we had been nearly starved to death and as there was no chance for other matter in the stomach of a hungry person. Therefore, as we could not think any other matter in our minds this time because of hunger, I did not waste time at all to climb this tree. I hardly climbed it to the top when I began to pluck the fleshy fruits on to the ground. Without hesitation, Aina, as she held my sword, began to collect the fruits in to one place under this tree.

When I was sure that I had plucked down about one hundred, I came down. Then we began to eat them one by one and we enjoyed them more than any other cooked food. Of course when a person was not yet hungry he would avoid many kinds of eatable things but it was not so for us this day in the forest, but we enjoyed these fruits of the wild mango even more than any of cooked food.

But as we were still enjoying the fruits there we heard unexpectedly that somebody was squabbling repeatedly as he was coming to us as quickly as he could. As soon as we glanced with fear at the direction from which we were hearing the horrible squabble, there we saw faintly at a long distance a fearful old man. He was coming to us with great anger as fast as he could. So without hesitation, both of us stood up and we stared at him with fear as we held the fruits which we were eating and I also held my sword firmly this time.

But as we were still trying our best to see him clearly just to make sure whether he was a human being or a dangerous forest spirit. He had come nearer with his squabble which was shaking the ground like a strong lightning. As soon as he was visible to us, we saw him clearly this time that he was not a real human being but we had not yet known what kind of a living creature he was. He had about six followers who was following him. As he and his followers were at a distance of about two hundred yards from us, we saw that he was in front of them and all were coming to us directly immediately they saw us. When he and his followers came very closely to us, then we saw him clearly this time that he was the Spirit of Fire. But as he was in front of his followers he shouted greatly with anger and as he opened his mouth very widely and shouted on us, a large quantity of big fire was sparking out from it and it (fire) was spilling upon us continuously. This fire was burning us so much that Aina and I did not know when we began to shake our bodies so that the sparking fire might be missing us.

As both of us were still shaking our bodies to left and right just to avoid the fire, yet we managed to look at this fearful creature and we saw him clearly that his head was three times bigger than his body and it was about six feet long and taper towards the end. The whole head was curved a little bit towards his back. As it was a little bit curved towards his back, it was so both edges of it had many long and wide feathers which were also curved together with the head. His nose was thicker than a round pillar of about three feet diameter and it was so much curved like a sickle that it was touching his chest. Each of his ears was as big as a big hat. Both his eyes were at the point where his curved head started. Each was seeing faintly in his skull and it was sparking out fire continuously to all directions to which he was turning his head.

His lower jaw was also large and was so much curved up that it was touching his forehead. But both his tongue and teeth were exposed for his wide mouth was permanently opened. Furthermore, his mouth was opened throughout the day and night in respect of his non-stop squabbles and the fire which was sparking out from it continuously. His neck was very thick with uncountable of thick veins which were surrounded it like that of a big tree. All of these veins were rested on both his shoulders, chest, etc. Each of his arms was longer and thinner than it should be. But each of his palms was as flat as a flat hand-fan but it was thicker than a plank of two inches. Each of the five fingers on each of his palms was very long and the nail on each was about eight inches long. His chest was as thin as a string. Both his thighs down to the toes had no shape at all. Each was long like a stilt and it seemed as if there was no flesh but bone.

From his taper head down to his feet was entirely fire. He and his followers were in the same form but his own appearance was more terrible. He was so old and dried up that if it was not for his terrible shout, squabbles, movements, etc., there would be nobody who might see him would believe that he was a living creature.

As soon as he and his followers came nearer to us this morning, they stopped at a distance of about ten yards

from us. But as Aina and I were about to start to run away
for our lives. This cruel Spirit of Fire moved his mouth
and shouted greatly on us. His shout was so fearful that
we could not run away as we had been trying to do.
Because as he shouted terribly on us a large quantity black
smoke was then rushing out from his mouth and it covered
both of us at the same moment. And without hesitation,
as he and his followers stood on the same spot and as he
held a heavy club of bone with both hands and raised it
above his curved head, he began to tell us loudly with
great anger: "You these two squanderers are certainly
perished today! Hah, I say, whosoever you are, you are
certainly perished this day. I shall take both of you to my
town, the town of fire, to be burnt into ashes because you
have eaten my fruits!" this Spirit of Fire shouted on us
like that as he was wheezing with extreme anger.

When he paused and thought what he wanted to do for
a while and then he squabbled with anger for some
minutes, he continued to shout with extreme anger: "You
these two human beings, probably you don't know who
I am! Let me tell you first what I am before I shall take
you to my town! I am the Spirit of Fire, the most cruel
creature on earth! I am the owner of the fire with which
the people of the world cook their food, etc. Without me,
there would no fire for the human beings to use, yet the
human beings hate me. But for the hatred they have on
me, I am so cruel and merciless to them that I used to
send great fire to every part of the world to burn uncountable houses, property, etc., everyday! As I hate the
water it is so I hate the human beings because they use
the water to quench my fire whenever it is burning them
or their houses, property, etc! Although the water was

first created and I was the second who was created by the Creator! As I am a living creature of fire it is so the water has its own living creature who is the goddess of the river or Nymph. As I am cruel to the human beings it is so I am kind to them in some ways but instead to be kind to me in return they take my kindness as an odium. Although the water is kind to the human beings and many other living creatures but thousands of them are drowned in it a year and their houses, property, etc., etc., are damaged also by it every year and I shall not forget to remind you of that! I am living in the greatest fire which is near this place and which is under the mountain of desperation. My followers who are uncountable and are cruel and merciless like myself are my messengers whom I am sending to all parts of the world to destroy the human beings' blongings!

"And it is so the Goddess of River who is living in the largest river or ocean with her messengers is sending out her messengers to damage as well the human beings' blongings! I have been living inside this mountain of desperation since the beginning of the earth and it is so for the Goddess of River! Now, to remind both of you again about my fruits which you have eaten. I am taking you to my town of fire which is in the biggest fire and there you will be burnt into ashes within a second! Please, my followers, push them along to my town!" When this cruel and merciless Spirit of Fire told us his story like that as the thick black smoke was rushing out from his mouth and the fire was also sparking out continously from the same mouth so much that every part of that place caught fire and within a few minutes the fire became a big flame.

He hardly related his story to us with various fearful

46

voices when he bent forward, he lifted the heavy club of bone which he held firmly with right hand above his curved head and then he started to come to us slowly to grip us with the left hand which was also sparking out a large quantity of fire continuously as he stared at us with his fearful eyes. Having seen this his fearful attitudes, Aina and I became extremely feared that we did not know when we twisted together when the fear could not allow us to run away for our lives. At this moment we did not know whether both of us were still alive or dead.

But as the hand of this Spirit of Fire was nearly to touch us. The Creator Almighty was so good that it came to my mind unexpectedly this time to cut his hand of fire with my sword perhaps he and his followers or messengers would run away. But as I lifted up the sword and cut his hand with all my power and fear. He stopped suddenly in one place as he drew his left hand towards his body. Without hesitation he then ordered four of his followers to come and push us to him. As soon as they came to us and as they were preparing to push us to him, I began to cut them continuously with my sword, but the sword could not do anything to them.

However, when they overpowered me, Aina and I surrendered ourselves to them, then without hesitation, they pushed us to their cruel master, the Spirit of Fire. So we stood before him but at a little distance from him and then we were trembling with fear. When he stared at us for a while with anger and as he was still squabbling and the thick black smoke was rushing out in large quantity from his mouth with the fire which was sparking out from the same mouth and was spilling on us continuously. He shouted greatly: "I shall not kill you here but I

47

shall take you to my town first before I shall burn you into ashes! All right, my followers, be pushing them along to my town now!" This Spirit of Fire hardly shouted like that to his followers when they began to push us roughly along to his town of fire which he said was under the mountain of desperation.

As his followers were still pushing us roughly along in this forest and as he himself was following them with his great and fearful non-stop squabbles, all of the nearby trees, weeds, etc., began to burn at the same time because the fire of his mouth which was spilling on them was very powerful. Having seen this, then I began to think in mind that probably this was the end of our lives. It came to my mind as well this time that although my father and mother had died in poverty but Aina and I were going to die in fire now.

As I was still lamenting in mind like that they pushed us to one strange mountain. The mountain was at a distance of about four miles to the place that they had caught us. This mountain was about six miles high and was about forty miles circumference. It was the mountain of desperation under which this Spirit of Fire, his followers and the uncountable creatures of fire lived. This Spirit of Fire was their king. There were no trees or any other kinds of plants which were grown on either side of this mountain of desperation. Because it was so dried that there was no any kind of plant which could grow out of it. There was very thick smoke which was rushing out in large quantity continuously from the inside of this mountain through its top to the sky. This kind of thick black smoke was so much thick that it could be held with the hand like a hard thing. So when Aina and I saw this strange thick

48

black smoke, we believed at the same time that there was no doubt, a great fire was inside the mountain.

As soon as the followers of the Spirit of Fire pushed us roughly to this mountain of desperation, they stopped. Then without hesitation, their master, the Spirit of Fire, knocked at a part of the mountain heavily for several times as he was still squabbling continuously. He knocked at that part so heavily that both the mountain and the land which was surrounded it shook heavily as if they were going to sink down. So Aina and I were so feared that we staggered to a distance of about quarter of a mile before we could stop ourselves but two of his followers ran to us at the same time and both of them pushed us back to their master. We were hardly pushed before him when he shouted greatly on us and said: "I say, both of you are certainly perished this day! You squanderers! I am going to burn you into ashes very soon!"

But as he shouted the fire which sparked out from his mouth, which was opened permanently, spilled upon us and then the clothes which were on our bodies caught fire at the same moment. But of course, the fire was quenched as soon as we fell down and began to roll to left and right on the ground for the pain.

As both of us were still rolling about on the ground a part of this mountain at which he knocked was opened unexpectedly by somebody who we did not see clearly. Then without hesitation, his followers pulled us up from the ground and they continued to push us roughly along the narrow path which went into this mountain as the Spirit of Fire, their master, was following them. Having travelled about two miles on this narrow path, there we came to a big town. This town was so big that it seemed as if it had no end at all. The millions of the creatures who were living there were that of the form of this Spirit of Fire, who was their king. Both children and adults were just like fire. Their houses were beautiful but the walls, roofs, etc., were fire as well. Their domestic animals like dogs, goats, sheep, horses, fowls, etc., each of them was just like that of the earthly domestic animal but it was fire in form.

As soon as they pushed us to this town of fire, they did not stop but they were still pushing us along roughly in the town until they pushed us to one mighty building of fire. It was the most beautiful building in this town and without hesitation they pushed us in. But very soon, Aina and I understood that this building was the palace of the Spirit of Fire because he was the king of this town. But as he was following us in to his palace as he was still squabbling loudly with great anger, thousands of trumpeters stood up and as soon as all of them bowed down for him they began to flatter him with their trumpets of fire until he went deeply into the palace and then sat down on his throne of fire before they stopped flattering him with the trumpets. Although everything was fire in this town but the fire did not burn or hurt anything unless when the Spirit of Fire himself commanded it to burn or hurt things.

When the followers of the Spirit of Fire pushed us just a little distance from the main entrance of the palace, they pushed us into one room which was at the left near the entrance. Although this room had no door but there was a very strong guard who began to keep watch on us as soon as the followers of the Spirit of Fire had told him that they caught us from the forest when we were eating the fruits which belonged to their master, the Spirit of Fire.

It was like that Aina and I were brought to this town of fire by the Spirit of Fire just the following day that we were narrowly escaped from the Chief Idol Worshipper who wanted to sacrifice us to his idol. Although I still held the sword which I took from the shrine of the Chief Idol Worshipper but these creatures of fire did not regard sword as of an important weapon. But of course they had no any other weapon more than their fire which their king, the Spirit of Fire, could command any time to burn even a mighty rock into ashes within one second.

Aina and I were in this room for good three days without eating anything and the guard who was detailed to be keeping watch on us did not bother whether we eat or not. But in the midnight of the fourth day that we were in this room. The Almighty Creator was so good, this guard fell asleep. Then without hesitation, as I held my sword, I whispered to Aina to follow me and she did so. So in the darkness, we escaped from the palace to another part of the town. Having tried all our efforts to go out of this town entirely before daybreak but were failed. Then we went to the outskirt of the town, we hid ourselves in the ashes. The ashes were as high as a high hill.

It was like that we buried ourselves alive in the ashes for many days as the followers of the Spirit of Fire were searching for us in both day and night. But we were very lucky that they could not find us out till one morning, when a heavy rain came. This rain was so heavy that within one hour its torrent carried the whole ashes together with us to a large river which was very far away from this town of fire.

As the torrent was carrying us away it was so we were trying all our best to come out of it but all our efforts were failed. But when we were tired then we left ourselves to be carrying us along. As soon as it carried us to this large river we sank into the bottom of the river. But we were very surprised to see that we could walk about in the bottom of this river as freely as we did on the land. But of course there was no water except dry white sand.

Then after Aina and I sat down on the sand and rested for some minutes. We stood up and then we began to roam about, we were looking for the road on which we could travel back to our village or to another town else. But as we had drunk much of the torrent as it was carrying us along to the river we did not feel hunger as before. Therefore, we could walk as fast as we wanted to but with great fear perhaps we might fall into the hand of another cruel creature again.

After a while, we saw a beautiful big house afar. Then with fear, we went direct to the house but unfortunately the main entrance of this house had been closed at that time. But as we stood at the entrance we were hearing that thousands of people were singing loudly with a lovely voice and they were also laughing and clapping with happiness. So this made it clear to us that the inhabitants of this beautiful house were in merriment and that they were kind creatures. But of course we had not yet seen them with eyes probably they were human beings like us or the gods of this river, we were not certain this time.

Having stood before the entrance for about an hour, one of them came out from the house with a smiling face. She was a woman of about forty years old. As soon as she saw both of us standing at the entrance, she came nearer with her smiling face. Without opening the big door of the entrance she first asked from us with a cheerful voice that from where we had come and how we had managed to be there. But she hardly asked these questions from us when I explained to her without fear that: "We were the captives of the Spirit of Fire who is the king of the town of fire. He captured us from the forest as the thieves of his fruits. But when he and his followers took us to his town to be burnt into ashes in respect of his fruits which we ate. We escaped from his custody in the night and we hid in the ashes for many days so that he might not be able to catch us again otherwise he would burn us into ashes immediately. But as we were still hiding in that ashes when a heavy rain came and without hesitation its torrent carried us to a big river and then we sank into the bottom of it. So we began to roam about until we have reached this your beautiful house." It was like that I explained to this beautiful woman.

I hardly explained to her how we came there when she opened the door of this entrance with smiling face. Then she asked us to follow her as she was returning to the house and we followed her with bravery. She took us to an old woman who sat on one beautiful throne. Then Aina and I stood before her as the woman who brought us to her sat down on a chair which was on the left.

There was a very beautiful crown on the head of this old woman. The crown was made of various kinds of attractive tiny beads. This old woman was dressed in beatiful garments which were quite different from that of the earthly garments. So according to her dress, we understood that she was the Queen or the Nymph of this big river. We met so many beautiful women who were well dressed and sat round her. And it was so many beautiful young ladies who were also well dressed were dancing and singing round her. After a while, we understood that the woman who brought us to her was her police.

As soon as we were brought in to this house and as we stood before the Queen of the River with the rags which were on our bodies and which were entirely soaked and as I held my sword. She asked from us: "How both of you had managed to come to my town?" But I explained to her with a cheerful and fearless voice as I had explained to the woman (her police) who brought us to her. "Both of you were carried to this my town by the torrent from the town of the Spirit of Fire?" she asked from us with wonder as the other women were kept quiet and were looking at us with wonder as well. "Certainly!" I replied at the same moment. When I replied to all of her questions, she stopped to rock to and fro on her throne. But she and the other women shouted together: "Ah, both of you were very lucky that the king (Spirit of Fire) had failed to find you out before the heavy rain came otherwise he would burn you into ashes with his fire! He is a merciless creature of fire!"

When the Queen and her women told us like that, she waved hand to us to sit down on a settee which was at a little distance from her throne. But as she noticed that we were anxious to eat by that time, she told her police-woman to give us food and drinks. As we began to eat the food with greediness, she told us that the Spirit of Fire was her enemy because he was too cruel to every kind of living creature. She assured us as well that she would take us back to him as soon as we had finished with the food and the drinks just to revenge on him for the punishment which he had given us.

54

The Spirit of Fire

But Aina and I were so much afraid that we stopped eating that food when the Queen told us that she would take us back to the Spirit of Fire to revenge on him. We began to beg her not to take us back to him but she told us that we should not be afraid at all. Then we continued to eat the food.

Having finished with the food and we drank to our satisfaction the Queen stood up, she told two of her policewomen to follow her to one private room which was not far from her throne. After a while, she and the two policewomen came back. But before they came out, she had changed her dress except her two policewomen who were still in their usual uniform. When she came out from the private room together with her policewomen. She told them to wait for her, again she and two of the women who sat near her throne all the while entered another private room which was opposite the first one. After a while, she and the two women came out, each of these two women was entirely covered with white small cowries except her eyes which were appeared faintly under the cowries and she carried one big pitcher which was full of water.

Immediately they came out from that room, the Queen told the whole of us to follow her and all of us did so. The Queen was in front, the two women who carried the pitchers of water, followed her, then Aina and I followed these two women while the two policewomen were following us at back. It was like that all of us were following the Queen to the town of the Spirit of Fire. But it was a great surprise to Aina and I to see that within five minutes the whole of us reached that town. Hardly entered this town when the Queen was going directly to the palace of the Spirit of Fire without fear and the rest of us were following her. But when it remained about one thousand yards to reach the palace, the Spirit of Fire had been informed by his gate-keeper that the Queen of the River, his enemy, was coming to his palace with her followers.

As soon as the Spirit of Fire had been informed that the Queen of the River and her followers were coming to him, he hastily equipped himself and his cruel followers with strong fire and then all of them came out. They met the Queen, etc. in front of his palace. Having seen him and his followers like that, the Queen and her followers, Aina and I stopped and the Spirit of Fire and his followers stopped as well at a little distance from the Queen. The two women who carried the pitchers of water put them down on the ground, the two policewomen stood closely to the Queen. Then the Queen herself held Aina and I with left and right hands and she put us in front of her.

Without hesitation, the Queen asked solemnly from the Spirit of Fire: "Why did you bring these two poor human beings from the forest to your town?" When the Queen asked this question from him, he became extremely annoyed and he shouted greatly as a large quantity of fire was sparking out from his mouth: "What? You have no right at all to ask such a nasty question from me! You hopeless Queen of the River! Go out from my town now otherwise I shall burn you and your followers into ashes now!" But the Spirit of Fire hardly shouted like that when he began to squabble as all of his cruel followers were looking at him anxiously to use his power without delay.

"Hold on, the Spirit of Fire! You know, I am the Queen

of the River. I am gentle and I am not harming or killing or punishing the human beings or the other creatures. But I am kind to all of them. I am even so kind that I am giving many of my children to all barren women who come to me! So, I am sure that I am powerful more than you!" The Queen of the River explained to the Spirit of Fire with a smile.

"You are telling lies, the Queen of the River! You can live only in the river. But I am so cruel and bold that I am living in the great fire, therefore, I am powerful more than you! Better you go back to your river now otherwise I shall burn you and your followers into ashes unexpectedly. Hah, fire! The great fire in which I live, in which I enjoy my life, in which my town is! The great fire which I can command and which obeys my command as if it is a living creature! Hah, fire! fire! the great fire! Please, the Queen of the River, go away from my town now!" the Spirit of Fire shouted like that on the Queen of the River for about one hour as the large quantity of fire which was sparking out from his mouth continuously was spilling upon the Queen of the River, her followers, Aina and myself.

The Spirit of Fire hardly boasted like that when he was preparing to burn the Queen of the River with his fire. But as soon as he moved his wide mouth and the thick black smoke rushed out so much that it was spread unexpectedly over the Queen, her two women who were in cowries and who carried the pitchers of water, her two policewomen, Aina and myself, that all of us were unable to see each other any more. Then meanwhile, the Queen of the River hastily commanded her two women who carried the two pitchers full of water to throw these two pitchers on to the Spirit of Fire and his followers.

When the pitchers were thrown on them they (pitchers) broke into pieces. But the water in these two pitchers was hardly touched and soaked the Spirit of Fire and his followers when the flood-tide came suddenly. This flood-tide was so powerful that it carried the Spirit of Fire, his followers, his town, etc. away at the same time. So the Queen of the River, her two women, her two police-women, Aina and myself were now floating along on top of this flood-tide instead to sink down. It was like that the whole of us sat on top of the flood-tide as it was carrying us along. After a while, this wonderful strong flood-tide was divided into two suddenly. The Queen of the River, her two women who were covered with cowries and who carried the two pitchers of water and her two policewomen, were carrying along to the river in which they were living by one part of that flood-tide. But Aina and I were carried back by the second part of the flood-tide to the fruit tree from where the Spirit of Fire and his followers caught us before we escaped from his town of fire.

As soon as this flood-tide carried us to the fruit tree, it dried up suddenly. But as soon as Aina and I found ourselves on the dry land under that fruit tree and as we stood up and were still wondering to see that we came back to this fruit tree once more. We saw the Queen of the River and her followers far away from us. All of them sat on top of the flood-tide. They were singing the song of the river with a very cheerful voice, they were beating the drums and were dancing, they were waving hands to us as they were bading us goodbye. But to our surprise and fear was that as we stood up under the fruit tree and we were dancing to their lovely song and drums, the whole of them disappeared unexpectedly. We saw them no more and also the flood-tide.

When the Queen of the River and her followers were disappeared and their song and the sound of their lovely drums were faded away, Aina and I stopped to dance at the same time. Meanwhile, we began to look round that place because all of what had happened to us was just like a dream to us. Having waited under this fruit tree until when we came back to our senses. Then without hesitation, we began to travel along to the east of this forest with fear of not being caught again by the Spirit of Fire because we were not sure whether he and his followers were still alive. But of course my long sword was still in my hand. That was how we were saved from the Spirit of Fire by the kind Queen of the River.

THE CRUEL KING

A cruel man cannot change another man's destiny.
A born and die baby makes the doctor a liar.
A barren woman is jealous of a mother.
A lazy man is jealous of a worker.

*

So as soon as we had left that fruit tree, we began to travel along towards the direction that the sun was appeared (east) from this forest. We did so perhaps we might see the road which went to a village or a town so that we might travel on it to that village or town.

But of course we were very lucky that we did not travel very far when we came to one rough road. Then with gladness, we began to travel on it to the east as well. Having travelled for about two hours we came to a town. This town was strange to us because we did not know anybody there. However, as we were hanging about, I saw one young man who was the same age with me. I greeted him as he wanted to enter a house. He stopped and came nearer to us at the same time. Then as he stood before us he replied cheerfully to my greeting. When I noticed that he was kind to the strangers like us, then I spoke to him in a friendly manner that I was in poverty so that I wanted to stay in that town with my sister, Aina, to be working there until when I would get sufficient money to be taken back to my village.

The cruel king

When I explained to this young man like that, he asked for my name first and I told him that my name was Ajaiyi. Then he told me that his own name was ADE, THE TRAITOR. But I did not know what he meant by "traitor" of course I shrank up with fear when he mentioned the word "traitor" together with his real name. However, as I believed that "a cruel man cannot change another man's destiny" I did not fear him so much whether, in future, he could betray me. So after he discussed with me about this town for some minutes, he asked us to follow him and we did so. He took us to his house which was not so far from the place that he met us. As soon as he gave us seats in his sitting room, he gave us the food and water. Having eaten together with him to our satisfaction, but as his house was so small that it could not contain both Aina and myself together with him and his wife. He took us to one nearby house. This house was small as well and it was empty but it could contain more than four persons. He told us to be living in it. After that he went back to his own house.

When it was about five o'clock in the evening he came back to us with food and two kegs of the native drink. Having satisfied ourselves with the food, then Ade, my new friend, began to enjoy ourselves with the drink as I was telling him more about my poverty which I had inherited from my father. I told him about the kidnapper who kidnapped Aina and myself to another town and then sold us to the slave-buyer who was the Chief Idol Worshipper of that town. I explained to him further before the drink was finished, that the kidnapper first deceived us that he was our eldest brother whose name was often mentioning to us, before my father died,

"Remember The Day After Tomorrow." The kidnapper first deceived us also that he was born by my father but he went to another town before Aina and I were born. I explained to Ade as well that if the kidnapper had not first deceived us like that he could had not been able to kidnap us. I was still intoxicated by the drink when I remembered this time to tell Ade as well about the cruel Spirit of Fire who wanted to burn us into ashes and also about the kind Queen of the River who saved us from the Spirit of Fire. Ade wondered greatly when he heard of all these difficulties which we came across before we came to his town.

But as "a born and die baby makes the doctor a liar" I could not say whether Ade believed all what I explained to him because he was not present when all happened to us.

As soon as Ade and I had finished the drink, he went back to his house to sleep because it was then nearly eleven o'clock in the night. Ade reluctantly went back to his house by that eleven o'clock, he wanted to remain with us till midnight but he feared the hunters who were keeping watch of the town and who might catch him as a thieve. When he left, Aina spread the mats on the floor, both of us laid down and then fell asleep immediately because we were very tired before reaching this town.

By six o'clock in the morning, Ade came in and woke us. As soon as Aina and I sat up on the mats, he told me that as I was in a great poverty which was driving me about, he would help me to get a job to do for some months. Ade explained to me further that if I could do the job I would get plenty of money to take to my village. I was extremely happy when Ade told me like that. Then without hesitation, I stood up, I hastily put on my trousers, etc. which had already been turned into rags and Aina put on her own dress which had already been turned into rags as well.

But as "a town is never so small as not to have a king or a ruler." So as this town had a king, Ade took us to him. Although this town was small. Ade hardly introduced us to the king (the cruel king) when I prostrated and Aina knelt down with great respect in front of the king. Ade told him that Aina and I were strangers who had just come to the town. So as I prostrated and Aina knelt down the king greeted us cheerfully, after that he warned us that he did not want thieves or lazy strangers in his town. When he warned us like that, I confessed to him that we were not thieves or lazy strangers but we were driving about by the poverty which we had inherited from our father and mother before both of them died.

Having explained to the king like that Ade hastily told him that Aina and I were looking for job to do. So without hesitation, he told Ade to give me one cutlass and one hoe and after that to take me to his corn-field to clear the whole of it for him. The king said further that he would pay me a few pennies if I could clear the whole of it. But of course I reluctantly agreed to clear the corn-field for this king, because I thought in mind at the same time that the few pennies which he promised to pay for me could not free me from my poverty. However, I promised him that I would clear it for him, because I must not refuse to clear it for him otherwise he might tell his killers to kill me.

Then Ade gave me the cutlass and the hoe, after that he took me to the corn-field and Aina followed us. Although this corn-field was more than two acres but

Aina and I cleared the whole of it within a few days. Having cleared it, I went to him, I told him that I had cleared the whole of it with the help of my sister, Aina. He did not believe me when I told him that I had cleared the whole of it. So he stood up and followed me to the field but he was very surprised to see that in fact the whole of it had been cleared as I told him. Then he and I returned to his palace. But to my sorrow, this cruel king paid me only two shillings and six pence. Having received this money from him, I reluctantly prostrated and then thanked him with sorrow before I left his palace. As soon as I got out of his palace, I began to grumble as I was going back to the house that it was certain that I was created with poverty.

However, when I grumbled to the house, I gave this two shillings and six pence to Aina. I told her to use it for our food. But as Ade was trying all his efforts to get me the odd jobs which I was doing everyday, I had more interest in him than when Aina and I had just come to this town.

Gradually, I became well known to many people of this town. They were chatting with me whenever they saw me in the town because it was soon revealed to them that I was a hard working man. They even liked me more than Ade because he was lazy. But of course, as "a lazy man is jealous of a hard working man." So Ade began to jealous the likeness which these people had on me. Then as time went on, he became unfaithful to me, but of course this had not yet been revealed to me at all, but I was faithful to him in all respects.

But at that time as there was a king who reigned in this town and who gave me his corn-field which I cleared for him but he paid two shillings and six pence for me for the job. But as this king was extremely selfish and cruel to all offenders. So he reserved a bush in which all offenders were killed. This bush was at a distance of about two miles from the town. It was a terrible bush indeed to all offenders and there the fearful creature who had the voice of that of a human being lived. This fearful creature was a human dead body eater and he lived in the big deep pond which was somewhere in this dreadful bush. There was nobody in this town who was bold or brave enough to go near the pond for the fear of this powerful creature.

During one rainy season, Ade, the traitor, who was unfaithful to me, offended this cruel and selfish king. The offence was quite simple enough for another king to forgive him. But although Ade asked for pardon, this king refused entirely, for he had never pardoned an offender in his life. There was a big tree at the front of the palace to which every offender was tied until the day arrived that he would be killed. This big tree which was an enemy to the offenders, was in the open place so that the whole people of the town might be able to come there and pay their last visits to any offender tied up.

And Ade was tied up to this tree and then the whole people of the town came to pay him their last visits until the very day that he would be killed reached. Everyone of these people was thankful to the king that he sentenced Ade to death, because he had been unfaithful to most of them. But as I was faithful to him and as it was a great sorrow to me if he was killed although he was unfaithful to me. I was trying all my best to see that he was released by the king. Yet all my efforts were failed, for this cruel king did not listen to my plea at all.

E   65

However, when Ade was taken to that dreadful bush by the king's killers, I followed them, because "an upright man should not copy unfaithful man." And in my presence Ade was beaten to death, as that was the order that the king had given to the killers.

But as I was a faithful friend to Ade and I liked him as well as I liked myself, I did not follow these killers back to the town. But I sat down near the dead body of my friend, Ade, which lay roughly on the ground. As I sat down near his dead body it was so I was driving away all the flies which were trying to cover the body. And it was so I was weeping bitterly for the death of my friend. My intention was to remain with his dead body until I too would be killed by a wild animal or a spirit. And I was still weeping loudly when a creature came to me from the place that I did not know. This strange creature had the voice of that of human being and his appearance was that of an ape but he had two long sharp horns on head. His arms were so much short that both could not even reach his breast bone and each of the arms had so many long fingers. He was human dead-body eating creature who was living in the deep pond which was somewhere in this dreadful bush.

Immediately he came unexpectedly, he told me: "Will you please leave this place now! I want to eat this dead-body; it is my food!" When this creature shouted terribly on me like that I began to beg him with a trembling voice not to eat it. I explained to him with tears as I was trembling with fear: "This dead-body is my friend whose name was Ade and he was the only man that I liked most in this world before he was beaten to death here by the king's killers. Therefore, you this creature, spare his dead-

body for me." "Do you believe that he was truly faithful
to you before he was killed here?" this terrible creature
asked quietly. "Yes, indeed, he was faithful to me," I
confirmed quietly. "All right," the creature replied calmly
together with the shrug of the shoulders. "If it is so, take
this small gourd, when you remove its cork put some of
the juju-powder which is inside of it on to your friend's
both eyes and he will become alive at the same moment.
But I do not believe you at all that this your friend was
faithful to you when he was alive, and as you do not allow
me to eat his body now, it will be revealed to you in the
near future that he was not faithful to you in all respects.
Even perhaps he may be the one who will cause your death
at last!" this terrible creature pointed finger to me and
warned me seriously with great anger and then he disappeared suddenly.

The small gourd which he gave to me was vomited
from his stomach. And when he disappeared suddenly, I
was in a great embarrassment because I could not decide
whether this creature was a spirit or not. I did not know
that he was the dead-body eating creature whose voice was
similar to that of human being and who was living in the
pond which was somewhere in this dreadful bush. But of
course I did not know that it was my weeping called him
out of the pond, the place of his abode.

However, as soon as he disappeared, I removed the cork
of this gourd and then I put some of the juju-powder which
was inside it on to both eyes of my friend, Ade. But to my
greatest surprise Ade woke up from the dead at the same
time and he began to talk to me as if there was nothing
happened to him. Then without hesitation, I corked this
juju-gourd back, I put it in my pocket so that he might

not see it. Because the terrible creature warned me seriously before he disappeared that I must not let Ade see or know the uses of it. As soon as Ade woke up from the dead and he became normal, both of us went back to the town with happiness. So as the people, the king's killers and the king himself, were still wondering to see Ade that he came back to the town alive, he hastily went direct to his house and I too went direct to the house in which Aina and I were living as well. That was how I saved Ade, the traitor.

When I entered the house I hung this juju-gourd on the rack in my room. So as from that day, whenever a person died in the town or in any village, I was the one who would be called to wake that dead person and a large sum of money was paid to me as the reward of my wonderful work. Very soon I became well known to all of the people and to the king of this town, that I got the juju which could wake the dead person. But as I was faithful to Ade was that I always gave a half part of the money that I received to him but he was not pleased with that. Instead he was worrying me everyday to tell him how to use this juju-powder but I refused entirely to tell him.

But as the terrible creature who had given me this wonderful juju-gourd told me that day that Ade was unfaithful to me. It happened one day that after I left this town for another place for only a few days. Ade went to my room, he took this juju-gourd from the rack and he hung an inferior gourd on it. The inferior one that which he hung there was so much resembled my own that it was very difficult to know the difference of it between my own which he took. Then he hardly took it from the rack when he went to a large river which was flowing into

68

the pond in which the terrible creature was living. He hardly threw it in that river when it carried it to the pond and then the terrible creature took it as it was floating about on the pond. He then swallowed it at the same time and then he waited for the day when he would appear to me again to ask it from me.

As soon as Ade threw this juju-gourd into the river, he went to the same cruel king who condemned him to death before I woke him. He told the king: "Your worship, I bring this secret news to you. Ajaiyi, my friend, who woke me last time when you condemned me to death, had told me that whenever any one of your family dies, he would not wake him, just to revenge on you because you condemned me to death last time." Having heard this bad news from Ade, the king grew annoyed and he kept this news in mind.

Of course I did not tell Ade such a secret news as this at all but he really told this lie to the king so that he might kill me because I did not tell him the uses of the juju-powder.

A few days later, I returned with happiness from my journey, and Ade came to my house, we drank together for many hours but he did not show it in his behaviour that he had betrayed me and I too did not know that my juju-gourd had been thrown into the river and that the one which was resembled it was hung on the rack by Ade.

A few days after that I returned from my journey, one morning, Aina and I sat down and we counted the money which I had saved and it was two hundred pounds. So with happiness, I told Aina that we were now free from our poverty which we had inherited from our father and mother before they died. And as I told her with happiness as well that we would return to our village with the money in a few days time. Having told Aina like that and she bursted into a great laughter, I went into the room, I kept the two hundred pounds in my box. But I hardly came out of the room when Ade entered. He told me that one of the king's family had just died by an accident and that the king sent him to come and call me for him.

Without hesitation, I ran to the king to hear what he wanted me for. But when I met the king in his palace, he begged me with a trembling voice and tears to help him wake his prince who had just died by an accident. And without a word, I went back to the house. I hastily took that inferior gourd from the rack which I supposed to be my own. When I returned to the king, I hastily removed the cork just to put the juju-powder on to the eyes of the dead family. But to my fear, it was sand which came out of it instead of the real juju-powder. In short, I failed to wake the prince. But as Ade was a traitor and unfaithful friend, he did not allow me to say anything when he started to ask me before the king: "Ajaiyi, have you not told me the other day that, one day, you would revenge on the king for condemning me to death the other day!"

"Ade, when did I tell you so?" I asked from Ade with great anger. "Oh—ho!" Ade shouted greatly on me. "Because both of us are before the king, that is why you deny now that you did not tell me the other day that you would revenge on the king for condemning me to death the other day!" When I heard all this from Ade, I was so confused that I was simply looking on without knowing what to say again.

Now, the king was convinced of the truth of the lies

which Ade told him. So without hesitation, this cruel king ordered his killers to take me to that dreadful bush and then to beat me to death. When the killers were taking me to that dreadful bush Ade followed them and he was making a mockery of me with great laughter along the road to the dreadful bush. And Aina, my sister, followed us as she was weeping repeatedly along the road. Having reached the bush, the killers and Ade beat me to death on the very spot on which he was beaten to death the other day before I woke him. When they beat me to death with clubs, the killers and Ade went back to the town but Aina did not go back with them. She sat before my dead body and then she began to weep loudly. Thus Ade, the unfaithful friend, betrayed me to death at last. And he hardly reached the town when he went to my room, he broke my box in which I kept my two hundred pounds. He took it away without leaving even one shilling for me.

A few minutes after the killers and Ade had left for the town, the very terrible creature who gave me the juju-gourd with which I woke Ade from the dead the other day, came there. Without hesitation, he woke me and then he asked for my friend—"Where is your friend, Ade, to-day?" "He is not here, he was even the very one who caused my death and he was even among the king's killers who beat me to death here with the heavy clubs," I wiped my face with both hands and then explained to this terrible creature with sorrow as Aina was looking at me.

"Did you not beg me the other day that Ade was faithful to you and that I must spare him for you?" this creature reminded me. "Certainly, I begged you that day to spare him for me and not to eat him. And it is true that I told you that day as well that he was faithful to me and that he was the only man that I liked most in this world," I replied with a dead voice.

"Now, I come back to you today but as you did not allow me to eat the dead-body of Ade the other day, I shall eat you today instead, because the human dead-bodies are my favourite food!" But as this terrible creature was preparing to kill me back and then to eat my dead-body. Aina hastily knelt down before him, she began to beg him with tears to spare me for her. She explained to him that I was her only brother that she got in this world and that it was the poverty which we had inherited from our father and mother was driving us about until we came to Ade's town. Luckily, when Aina explained like that to this terrible creature with tears which were rolling down her cheek, he hesitated for a few minutes and then he said: "All right, I reluctantly spare him for you because it is a pity to me to hear from you that he is your only brother and that both of you are in poverty! All right, both of you can go back to the town now but I warn you seriously that you should disassociate yourself from Ade forthwith otherwise he will soon run you into another trouble! Goodbye!" This terrible creature hardly spared me for Aina and warned me seriously when he disappeared suddenly.

Then Aina and I went back to the town with happiness and the people of the town including Ade, the traitor, were surprised to see that I returned alive. Of course, I woke Ade from death the other day when the cruel king condemned him to death for only a minor offence which was not deserved death sentence. But he betrayed me to death at last.

However, as soon as Aina and I entered the house I went direct to the room just to open the box in which I kept my two hundred pounds to take a few shillings from it which to be used for our food. But to my disappointment, I saw that the box had been broken into pieces and the two hundred pounds had been stolen away. Immediately I saw that the money had been stolen, I did not know when I fell down and fainted for about thirty minutes before I became normal. As soon as I became normal I went out I asked from a number of people whether they knew who had stolen my money. But they told me that they saw Ade when he entered the house and that he was the man who had stolen away my two hundred pounds. Having heard this information from the people I went to Ade. I asked him about the money but he denied entirely that he was not the one who had stolen it. When I tried all my efforts to recover the money back from Ade but were failed then I came back to the house with great sorrow and embarrassment. But I was quite sure that he was the right person who stole the money. That was how my two hundred pounds was stolen away by Ade, the unfaithful and traitor friend.

Now, I came back to my poverty as before. When I came back to the house, I sat down and then I began to say within myself that it was certain that I was really created with poverty otherwise Ade could have not been able to steal my two hundred pounds. Now I could not get such a big money as this again because the juju-gourd or magic gourd which had the power to wake the deads had been thrown into the river by Ade and the terrible creature who gave it to me, the terrible creature who had the voice that of the human beings, had taken it back as soon as Ade threw it into the river. It was this magic gourd which had fetched me the two hundred pounds.

Now, as the money had been stolen away by Ade, the traitor, and the juju-gourd or magic gourd had gone back to the terrible creature, the owner of it. I told Aina that we should leave this town in the following morning for our village. So in the following morning both of us left this town without even a half-penny in hand except the sword which I had taken from the shrine of the Chief Idol Worshipper who wanted to sacrifice us to his idol when the kidnapper sold us to him.

Having travelled for some days, luckily we came to our village in the midnight. So we opened the doors and windows and we swept the whole house. In the morning, a number of our neighbours came in and greeted us. They gave us food and many yams as well. But when it was the third day that we had arived in the village. All my creditors came to me, they asked me to pay their money which I owed them before Aina and I were kidnapped away from the village. These my creditors thought that I brought money from our journey, they did not know that it was only sword that I brought. But when I begged them for many hours to give me some days to pay their money, luckily they agreed and then they went back to their houses.

Within a few days that we had arrived in the village, Aina's old friend, Babi, heard that she had arrived in the village. She came to greet her and then both of them continued their friendship. Because both of them were loved each other since when they were children. They were wearing the same kind of clothes and were going together to everywhere in the village and to several

74

other villages as well. They were doing everything so much together that many people who did not know their parents thought that they were twins.

DON'T PAY BAD FOR BAD

~~~~~~

When there is a quarrel the song becomes an allusion.
It is the end that shows the winner.
Excessive jealousy makes a woman to become a witch.
Fretting precedes weeping; regret follows a
mistake; all the brain men of the country assemble
but they find no sacrifice which can stop a mistake.

*

Aina and Babi were still going about together until when they became old enough for marriage. But as they loved each other, they decided within themselves to marry to two men of the same family who lived together in the same house, so that they might be with each other always. Luckily, after a few days that they had thought to do so. They heard of two gentlemen who were born by the same mother and father and who lived in the same house as well. So Babi married to one of these two men while Aina, with my consent, married to the second one who was the senior. Now, Babi and Aina were extremely happy as they were together as well in their husbands' house as when they had not married.

A few days after their marriage, Aina cleared a part of the front of the house very neatly. She sowed one kola-nut on that spot. Within a few weeks this kola-nut shot out. Then Aina filled up one jar with water and put it in front of her new kola-nut tree. Every early in the morning she would go and kneel down before her tree and the jar. Then she would pray to the kola-nut tree and the jar to help her get baby in time. After the prayer, Aina would drink some of the water which was inside the jar, after that she would go back to her room before the rest people in the house woke. Aina was doing like that every early in the morning. Because she believed that there was a certain spirit who was coming and blessing the kola-nut tree and the water in the jar in the dead night.

After some months, the kola-nut tree grew up to the height of about two feet. But this time, the animals of the village began to eat the leaves of this new tree and this hindered its growth. One morning Babi met Aina, her friend, as she knelt down quietly before the tree and the jar and she was praying quietly. After she prayed and stood up just to enter the house, Babi asked: "Aina, what were you telling your kola-nut tree?" "Oh, this kola-nut tree is my god and I ask from it always to help me to get a baby in time," Aina pointed finger to the tree and the jar and she explained to Babi calmly.

But when Babi noticed that the animals of the village had eaten the leaves of the tree. She went back to her room. A few minutes later she brought out the head of her large pitcher, the body of which had broken off. She gave it to Aina and she told her to cover her kola-nut tree with it so that the animals might not be able to eat its leaves again. Aina took the head of the pitcher from her and she thanked her greatly. Then she covered her tree with it at the same time, however as from that morning the animals of the village were unable to eat the leaves of the tree and at this time it was growing as quickly as possible in the centre of the head of the pitcher.

After a few years, this kola-nut tree yielded the first kola-nuts. The first nuts that this tree yielded were of the best quality in the village. So in respect of that the kola-nut buyers bought the whole nuts with a considerable amount of money. And when this tree yielded the second and third kola-nuts, the buyers bought them with a large amount of money as before. In selling these nuts, Aina became a wealthy woman within a short period.

But as "when there is a quarrel the song becomes an allusion" and that "excessive jealousy makes a woman to become a witch", was that when Babi saw the large amount of money which Aina realized from her kola-nut tree, she was so jealous that one morning she asked: "Aina, will you please return the head of my pitcher to me this morning?" "What? The head of your pitcher?" Aina shouted with a great shock. "Yes! The head of my broken pitcher! I want to take it back from you this morning!" Babi replied with a jealous voice. "Well, the head of your broken pitcher cannot be returned this time unless I break it into pieces before it will be able to come out from the kola-nut tree," Aina replied with a dead voice.

"The head of my pitcher must not be broken into pieces nor split in any part before you will return it to me!" Babi shouted with the voice of quarrel. "I say it cannot be taken away from the tree unless the tree is cut down!" Aina explained loudly. "Yes, you may cut the tree down if you wish to do so. But at all costs, I want the head of my pitcher back now!" Babi shouted greatly on Aina. "Please, Babi, remember that both of us had become friends since when we were children. Therefore, do not try to take the head of your broken pitcher back this time!" Aina reminded Babi with a cold voice. "Yes, of course, I don't forget at any time that the two of us have become very close friends since when we were youths. But at any rate, I want the head of my broken pitcher back now!" Babi insisted with great dirty noise.

At last, when it revealed to Aina that Babi simply wanted to destroy her kola-nut tree so that she might not get the kola-nuts from it to sell again. Then she went to the court of law. She sued Babi for attempting to destroy her kola-nut tree. But at last, when the judge failed to persuade Babi not to take the head of her pitcher back from Aina. He judged the case in her (Babi) favour that Aina must return the head of her broken pitcher to her.

Then with great sorrow, the kola-nut tree was cut down and the head of the broken pitcher was taken from the stump of the kola-nut tree and was returned to Babi. Babi was now very happy but not in respect of the head of her pitcher but in respect of Aina's kola-nut tree which was cut down. Because she believed that Aina would not get the kola-nuts to sell any more.

After Aina's kola-nut tree was cut down and the head of Babi's broken pitcher was taken from the stump of the tree and was given back to her. She and Aina entered the house but as "it is the end that shows the winner", both of them continued their friendship. Because Aina did not show in her behaviour towards Babi that her tree which was cut down or destroyed was a great sorrow to her. But of course Aina believed that however it might be it was the end that would show the winner.

A few months after the kola-nut tree was cut down, Babi delivered to a female baby. In the morning that Babi's baby was named, Aina gave her one fine brass ring as a present, she told her to put it on her new baby's neck, because the brass ring was one of the most precious metals at that time. Babi took this brass ring from Aina with great admiration and with gladness, she put it on her baby's neck at the same time. So this brass ring added more beauty to her baby. This brass ring was carefully moulded without any joint.

Ten years passed away like one day, when one fine morning, as Babi's baby who was then a daughter, was celebrating her tenth birthday. Aina went in to Babi, she asked with a smiling face:

"Babi, my good friend, I shall be very glad if you will return my brass ring this morning."

"Which brass ring!" Babi jumped up suddenly and shouted.

"My old brass ring which is on your daughter's neck now!" Aina pointed finger to the neck of Babi's daughter as if she was simply joking with her.

"This very brass ring on my daughter's neck now?" Babi asked with embarrassment.

"Yes, please," Aina replied with a smile.

"Please, Aina, my good friend, don't try to take your brass ring back this time. As you know, before the ring can be taken away from my daughter's neck, her head must be cut off first because her head has already been bigger than the ring!" Babi began to beg with tears.

"I don't tell you to cut off the head of your daughter

but I want my brass ring back now without cutting it!"
Aina was now scowled at Babi and she insisted to take
her brass ring back.

At last when Babi failed to persuade Aina not to take
her brass ring back, she went to the same court of law.
She sued Aina for attempting to kill her daughter. But as
it was certain that "fretting precedes weeping; regret
follows a mistake or jealousy or wickedness; and as all
the brain men of the world assemble but they cannot
find the sacrifice which can stop a mistake", was that
although Babi sued Aina to the court of law for attempting to kill her daughter because she knew that
before Aina's brass ring could be taken away from her
daughter's neck, the head must be cut off first. But unfortunately, the case was judged in favour of Aina when she
related the story of her kola-nut tree to the judge how it
was cut down when Babi wilfully insisted to take the head
of her broken pitcher back ten years ago. In the judgment,
the judge added that the head of Babi's daughter should
be cut off in the palace of the king and in the presence
of the whole people of the village, so that everyone might
learn that jealous was bad. Then a special day to behead the
daughter was fixed.

When the day was reached and as the whole people
of the village had gathered in the palace of the king and
the king himself sat in the middle of the prominent people.
Then the king told Babi loudly to put her ten-year-old
daughter in the centre of the circle of the people and
she did so. She and her daughter stood and both were
trembling with fear as the swordsman, who was ready to
behead her daughter, stood at the back of her daughter
with the sword in hand and was just expecting to hear

the order from the king and then to behead the poor daughter.

The multitude of people were so quiet with mercy that it was after a few minutes before the king could reluctantly announce loudly to Babi: "Now, Babi, as Aina's kola-nut tree was cut down when you insisted to take the head of your broken pitcher back ten years ago, it is so the head of your daughter will be cut off now before Aina's brass ring will be taken away from the neck of your daughter and then it will be given back to her!" the king announced loudly and the multitude of people were mumbled with grief.

Then the king closed both his eyes and gave the order to the swordsman to behead Babi's daughter. Having heard this, Babi jumped up suddenly, she knelt down and she began to beg for pardon. But she had forgotten that: "fretting precedes weeping; regret follows a mistake; but when all the brain men of the world were once assembled together they could not find the sacrifice which could stop the mistake." But of course, as the swordsman raised the sword up just to cut the head off. Aina hastily stopped him and then she announced loudly: "It will be a great pity if this daughter is killed with a vengeance in respect of my kola-nut tree which was cut down when her mother, Babi, insisted to take the head of her broken pitcher back ten years ago. Her mother did that so that I might not get the kola-nuts to sell again. So, now, I believe, if we continue to pay bad for bad, bad shall never finish on earth! Therefore, I forgive Babi what she had done to my kola-nut tree!" Having heard this announcement from Aina, the king, prominent people and the multitude of people clapped and shouted loudly together for Aina. Then everyone went back to his or her house. But Aina and Babi were still good friends. Although Aina became poor soon after her kola-nut tree was cut down. But when the kola-nut tree was cut down and Aina could not get money again, I said within myself that both of us were really created with poverty.

But as Aina was with her husband with much difficulties and great poverty it was so I too were in difficulties as well. The difficulties in which I was, was that all my creditors were giving me much troubles to get the money that I owed them before Aina and I were kidnapped, from me. They troubled me so much that I was unable to rest or sleep in both day and night.

At last, when I could no longer bear these troubles, one day, I thought within myself to leave the village for wherever that I could get a kind of job to do probably I might get sufficient money so that I could be free from my poverty and to pay all my debts as well out of the money.

The following morning that this thought came to my mind, I went to Aina. I told her that I would leave the village the following morning for wherever I could get a job to do so that I might get money. Aina agreed at the same time because she knew that without going abroad to find a kind of job to do I could not get any money and she knew as well that if I stayed in the village longer than this time, my creditors would certainly kill me soon. Therefore, she wished me good-luck and safety return, but she said all this with tears.

Having bade good-bye to Aina with tears, I came back to the house. Then I sharpened one of my father's cutlasses, I kept it ready in the room. As soon as it was midnight, I woke up, I took the cutlass with my sword which was in a leather sheath. I hung it on my left shoulder and I hung my huge leather bag on the same shoulder as well. After that, I hastily left the village before daybreak so that my creditors might not see me otherwise they would not allow me to go without paying their money for them. It was like that I left my village to an unknown destination. But it was the poverty which I had inherited from my father and mother was driving me away from the village.

I VISITED THE CREATOR IN
RESPECT OF MY POVERTY

∽∽∽∽∽∽∽∽∽∽∽∽∽∽∽∽∽∽∽∽∽∽∽∽∽∽∽∽∽

*It is the place where three roads meet that
puzzles a stranger.*
*It is in the time of difficulties that one knows a
true friend.*

*

Very early in the morning I left my village as quickly as
possible so that my creditors might not see me. Having
travelled about one quarter of a mile to the village, I came
to where three roads met. But as "it is the place where
three roads meet that always puzzles the strangers." So I
stopped at the junction of these three roads because I was
so puzzled that I did not know on which of these three
roads to travel. But as there was a small hut on the centre
of the junction of these three roads which was built for
the Devil which the old people of my village were worshipping. I stopped, I knelt down before the Devil who
occupied the whole of the hut. I called out his titles and I
praised him with a cheerful voice to show me the right one
of these roads which to be taken. Because the Devil was so
important that we must regard him when going somewhere, etc.

As soon as I had regarded him it came to my mind to
take the road which was on the left. Then I stood up and
I began to travel along on it at the same time. When I

85

travelled on this road till about seven o'clock in the evening without reaching any town or village except the people who I did not know that I was meeting on the road. So when the darkness did not allow me to see the road again, I stopped, I sat down on the bank of the road. I cast down and then I fell asleep at the same time without fear, because I was very tired and hungry. It was like that I cast down and slept till daybreak. When it was daybreak, I woke up and I continued to travel along on this road without knowing the destination of it.

After I travelled about twenty miles, I came to a town at about two o'clock p.m. But as I was wandering about in this town with the hope that I might see one of the inhabitants who would be kind enough to allow me to stay in his house until I would get a job to do. But it was a great disappointment to me that every person that I saw and greeted in this town did not answer. For all of them thought that I was a mad man in respect of my dirty appearance especially the dirty rags which were on my body.

However, as I was still roaming about with shame of being in this my dirty appearance, I came to the extreme end of this town where there was a house. All of the walls of this house were almost cracked and all were nearly to fall down for lack of care. The roof was thatched with spear-grasses from a very long time because they were so old that most of them had been carried away by the breeze. Immediately I saw the house in this such a bad condition, I knew that the owner of it was as poor as myself. Now, without shame, I went to the entrance, I knocked at the door gently so that it might not fall down because it had already been dislocated from the cracked walls. After a while, two men who were on the same age with me, came from this house to the door. Both greeted me with the voice of that of a poor man. But as it is "Hardwords draw out the club or gun, but softwords bring the kola out from the pocket", was that I answered with great respect and with the voice of that of a poor man. Although when I looked at both of them very well, I saw that their own appearances were even worse than my own. Both of them were dirty more than myself and were in rags many parts of which were stitched together with ropes instead of thread because they had no money to buy the thread.

Having seen me in this poor condition like themselves, they did not hesitate to tell me to follow them to the inside of the house and I did so. When they took me to their sitting room they gave me one very old stool and I sat on it at the same time while both of them sat down on the floor because they had no other stools. But as they lifted their heads up and were expecting me to tell them what I came to them for. Then I explained to them that the poverty which I had been inherited from my father and mother before they died had forced me to leave my village. But as I was wandering from one place to another just to find a job to do to get sufficient money, the only thing which could set me free from my poverty and I had not yet got it, then I came to their town unexpectedly. When I explained to them like that with a sorrowful voice and yet I wanted to explain to them further how Aina and I were kidnapped and sold to the Chief Idol Worshipper.

Ojo and Alabi, as that were their names, did not allow me to finish my explanations when they waved hands to me to stop and I stopped at the same time. Then without hesitation, they explained their own poverty to me with tears. When the three of us wept bitterly together for some minutes in respect of our poverty, we stopped weeping and then we comforted ourselves that if the Creator spared our lives probably he might set us free from our poverty before we died. But as "It is in the time of difficulties and hardships that one knows a true friend" was that as soon as we comforted ourselves, Ojo and Alabi told me to stay with them instead of wandering about like a mad man. It was like that we three poor friends began to live together with sorrow.

As we were living together, it was so the three of us were working hard everyday. We were working even harder than any other young man of our age. But to our surprise, as we joined hands together and we were working hard it was so our poverty was growing worse than ever and our debts were becoming more and more everyday. And within six months our creditors were so many and were troubling us so much that we were unable to return from the farm to the town in the daytime except in the night when the darkness was not allowed them to recognize us. Now we became the recluses of our creditors.

But at last, when our debts and poverty came to the climax. One day, the three of us sat down and began to discuss within ourselves what we could do to ease this our hardship. As we were still suggesting whether to commit suicide, it came to our minds to go to the Creator by all means to beg him to set us free from this our poverty. When this thought came to our minds we put the day to leave the town for the Creator's town for eight days time. But it was extremely difficult to visit the Creator in his town, because his town was very far off. Even many people were saying that his town was not in this world. However, when the day was reached, everyone of us took his own cutlass, bow and arrows, etc., with which to fight the bad spirits, ghosts, etc. whenever we met them on our way.

We were going to travel in the jungles, bushes, forests, in the deep valleys, on high hills, etc. etc., for more than six months before, probably, we could reach the town of the Creator because there was no road on which to travel at all. So we left the town before dawn and we started our journey so that our creditors might not see us otherwise they would not allow us to go unless we paid their money. It was like that Ojo, Alabi and myself started our journey without a half-penny in hand but with rags on our bodies.

There was nobody who must go to the Creator's town twice. Even once a person had returned he would fear to go back because of the difficulties, hardships, punishments, etc. which he had met on the way for the first time he went there. And the people who were not extremely poor, etc. would never attempt to go there. By that time the way to the town was still opened for people to go there but alas! that way had already been closed and the people who are still alive could not visit him again. Why? Because the Creator hates the sins.

Having left the town before dawn, we travelled on the real road for seven days and then we came to the end of it. Now, we continued our journey from forest to the jungle, etc. As we advanced in this journey we were eating only ripen fruits whenever we were hungry for food. We were sometimes sleeping in the hole of a big animal when it was night. And it was so the bad creatures like spirits, elves, goblins, one legged ghosts, four legged ghosts, etc.

which we were meeting on the way in the jungle, were attacking us without mercy and it was so we too were fighting them stubbornly until we were winning them.

One day, in the second month that we had been travelling in one dreadful jungle, we met two strange creatures unexpectedly. These two strange creatures were one legged ghosts with one eye and one big ear on their heads. We had not met these kind of ghosts since when we had begun our journey. As soon as they saw us far away both of them left the direction that they were going but were coming to us as hastily as they could. When we saw them that they were coming to us and that their attitudes showed that they were bad ghosts, we branched to another direction and we were going as hastily as we could so that they might not be able to meet us. But as we branched to another direction they too branched to that direction. Having seen them did so we branched to the left but they too did so. Again, we branched to the right and we continued to go as quickly as we could perhaps they would go back from us but they too branched to the right and were coming to us even faster than before.

Having seen the fearful attitudes of these one legged ghosts which showed that they were coming to harm us. Then without hesitation, we began to run furiously along in this dreadful jungle which was the home of the harmful creatures. Having seen that we were about to lose to their view, they too began to chase us to catch at the same time and within a few seconds they overtook us. And without hesitation they held us as if we were thieves and then they began to box both our ears and faces repeatedly without mercy. After they boxed both our ears and faces with all their power to their satisfaction. They began to drag us along to where we did not know yet. When they dragged us along in this jungle for about two hours they came to their home which was under a mighty hill.

As soon as they dragged us into their house, we saw that one of them ran to one corner, he took one knife and one strong lont rope. When he brought them, both of them wanted to tie us up to one big tree which was near there and then to cut our necks with that knife. What they were just trying to do was that having cut away our necks they wanted to roast us from the fire and then to eat us. But when we understood what they wanted to do and as we were quite sure that "when the head is cut away from the neck, the body is entirely useless." We did not waste time at all to defend ourselves. I told Ojo and Alabi with bravery that however it might be, "a man never die twice but once." Therefore we must fight these two ghosts with all our power to save ourselves from them. I told Ojo and Alabi further that if these two ghosts could overpower us and kill us in their hole we should not mind or if we could try our very best and overpower them then we would continue our journey to the town of the Creator.

I hardly told Ojo and Alabi like that when the three of us held our cutlasses firmly and then we were ready to fight them. But when they came to us and as they were preparing to tie us to that big tree with the rope before they would cut our necks away. We started to cut them with the cutlasses repeatedly with all our power. As we were cutting them with the cutlasses it was so they too were boxing us with all their power. They were boxing us so heavily that we were falling down ten times in a second because they were as strong as a giant. This fight was so fiercely that we damaged both their house or

91

hole and all of their belongings within a few minutes although their powers were beyond that of the human beings. As our bodies were bleeding and sweating as if though we bathed it was so for them as well.

After a while, we were so lucky, they became tired. They were so tired that they fell down and began to struggle to die but of course they were immortal creatures. As soon as both of them fell down helplessly, we took all of their fighting weapons. After that we sat down, we rested for some minutes because we were extremely tired. Having rested for a while, we ate all of their food. Having satisfied ourselves with the food we took their fighting weapons and our own. Then we came out from their hole and we continued our journey at the same time in the same jungle. It was like that we were safe from these one legged ghosts.

But when we travelled for about seven days in this dreadful jungle we came to another one. Then we stopped, we hastily treated all the wounds which were inflicted on our bodies by these bad ghosts. Having done so, we did not attempt to continue our journey this day, because we were very tired. But in the following morning we did not hesitate to continue our journey in this new jungle without fear of being caught again by any other kind of a harmful creature.

When we travelled fast for about six miles without stopping to eat or rest, we came to the end of this new jungle. But unfortunately, as there was a very big deep river at the end of it, we stopped at the bank of this river. We gathered some edible nuts that which we could find around. We made the fire and roasted the nuts from it, then we ate them, after that we drank the water from the river to our satisfaction. But as there was no canoe or any other thing with which to cross this river to the other side, we waited at the bank. We began to think how we could cross it to the other side but we did not know how we could cross it till when the night came. At last, when we failed to cross it, we laid down on the bank and then we fell asleep at the same time.

But as we were still enjoying the sleep, it was hardly midnight when about fifty strange creatures came to us. As soon as they had surrounded us they began to kick us with all their power as they were shouting horribly on us with their topmost voices: "Wake up and let us beat you to death! You hopeless human beings! Wake up and let us beat you to death at once!" These strange creatures shouted greatly on us like that with great anger. So their horrible shouts were so fearful that we did not know when we woke from sleep and then we stood up and began to tremble from head to foot with fear. And as we were still trembling with fear we saw these strange creatures that they were a kind of harmful and merciless creatures of that river. They came out from this river and they hated the human beings so much that they killed them whenever they met or saw them. But we had not met these kind of strange creatures since when we had begun our journey in these jungles.

Each of them was not more than three feet tall but as thick as a stump of a big tree of about four feet diameter. They had the eyes and heads which were that of a fish but the thick long hairs were on their heads. They had long legs and arms which were quite different from that of human beings because their palms and feet had no fingers, all were just flat and thick. Their eyes were round

93

like a circle with a very powerful bright tiny light which were bringing out a very powerful beam of light to a distance of not less than six hundred yards. Their bodies which were shedding out cold water repeatedly had a big and long vein on each side. So these their appearances showed us that they were certainly the harmful and merciless strange creatures of this river.

So as these strange creatures of the river were very dexterous, we hardly woke and stood up with fear when all of them began to beat us as the powerful beam of light of their eyes was penetrated into our own eyes. As soon as this powerful light had been penetrated into our eyes we did not see again but these strange water creatures were still beating us repeatedly with all their power and without mercy as they were shouting horribly on us. But after a while, when they did not stop to beat us, we too started to cut them with cutlasses although we could not see exactly where they stood as soon as the beam of the light of their eyes had been penetrated into our eyes. But of course as we were blindly cutting any part of that spot that which we were hearing their shouts, we were sometimes mistakenly cutting each other instead of these creatures. But at last, when we could no longer bear the pains of their beats we began to move backward from them perhaps they would stop to beat us. As they did not attempt to stop beating us but they were moving towards us and were still beating us continuously as we were moving backward from them, we slipped into this river unnoticed.

So we hardly slipped into the river when these water creatures jumped into the river with gladness and then they continued to beat us mercilessly. When we felt the pains too much we dived into the bottom of the river perhaps they would stop to beat us. But they too dived at the same time and then continued to beat us. So without hesitation, when we were sure that they would soon kill us if we did not come out from this river as soon as possible, we forced ourselves to cross this river to other side. But as soon as we came out from the river at the other end, these water creatures ran to us and they continued to beat us. At last, when we saw that we could not overpower them in any way, we began to run along for our lives. To our fear, these strange water creatures were chasing us along and continued to beat us until when it was daybreak. But as soon as the sun was appeared it quenched the powerful beam of light of their eyes. Now we could see them clearly and then the three of us faced them. We began to cut them repeatedly with all our power and within a few minutes they ran back to their river with severe cuts on all over their bodies.

It was like that we defeated these harmful and merciless strange creatures of the river. But as we had now understood that it was only in the night they had power to use the powerful beam of light of their eyes, we did not wait to rest but continued to travel along as hastily as we could in this jungle so that we might be able to travel far away from that river before the night came. Having travelled far away from that river and we were quite sure that we were safe from them then we stopped. We ate the ripen fruits which we found near there, after that we sat down and leaned our backs on a big tree. As we were enjoying the cool breeze it was so the three of us were discussing about that strange creatures of the rivers because they were too strange to us. After a while, we did not know when the three of us fell asleep unexpectedly because we were very tired and again we had much pains all over our bodies because we were nearly beaten to death by that strange creatures of that river.

It was like that the three of us were sleeping from that morning without waking once till the midnight. But when it was midnight we heard suddenly the noises of many drums. Then we woke and stood up with fear. When we looked round we saw that seven drummers had already surrounded us before we woke. They were beating their drums in such a strange way that we did not know when we started to dance. As they were beating their drums it was so they were singing a kind of strange song with lovely voices in such a way that there was no any human being who might hear it would not dance with happiness.

Having danced for about one hour without knowing whether these drummers were going to kill us, they stopped to beat their drums and stopped to sing as well. As soon they stopped, they asked: "Where are three of you going to?" Alabi hastily replied that we were going to visit the Creator. Again, they asked: "What are you going to visit him for?" Ojo replied that we were going to visit him in respect of our poverty. Ojo explained further that we wanted the Creator to set us free from our poverty. Having heard these explanations one who was the head for the rest shook his head up and down and then he told us that they were the drummers and singers for the Creator. He told us as well that he would take us to the Creator.

When he told us like that we were afraid perhaps they were harmful creatures but when we thought over again that they were human beings like ourselves, we were very happy to follow them. Then he told us to be in front of them. As soon as we did so, he and his men began to beat their drums with a kind of a lovely song. So, Alabi, Ojo and I hardly heard the drums and song when the three of us began to dance along in front of them as they were following us behind. It was like that we were dancing along and they were following us till daybreak.

But when it was about eight o'clock in the morning, we came to a very wide and clean road which went to the town of Creator. This road was very attractive and was very straight. There was no any human being who might see it would not like to travel on it to the end.

As soon as we came to this lovely road and started to travel on it, these drummers of the Creator, changed the way that they had been beating their drums when we were in the jungle to another lovely one and they changed their song as well. But as they changed everything this time, it encouraged us so much that as we were dancing here and there on the road it was so we were shouting greatly with happiness. As we were still doing so along on the road we came to one big gate the door of which was closed the time we came there. But as soon as the gate-keeper heard the noises of the drums, he hastily opened the door and he asked us to go in. It was like that we danced to the town of Creator after we had spent about six months in the jungles with severe punishments which we received from the harmful and merciless creatures.

AT LAST WE REACHED THE TOWN
OF THE CREATOR

∞∞∞∞∞∞∞∞∞∞∞∞∞∞∞∞∞∞∞∞∞∞∞∞∞∞∞∞∞∞

> *A tortoise's shell is a house of the poverty*
> *and if the tortoise is taken to the wealthy*
> *town, it will still be living in its house*
> *of poverty.*

*

At last we reached the town of Creator. As soon as we entered this town, the drummers stopped to beat their drums and stopped to sing as well but they took us to one beautiful house. They asked us to sit and we did so. Then they left us there and went out but a few minutes later three beautiful ladies brought food and many kinds of drinks to us. After we ate to our satisfaction we washed our hands. But as we wanted to start to drink the drinks the drummers came back, they sat and all of us drank the drinks for about two hours.

Having finished with the drinks, they told us to follow them and we did so. They began to take us round the town and they were showing us all the wonders of this town which we had not seen in our lives. When it was about one o'clock p.m. they took us to their court of law in which we met many offenders who stood before the judge. The offences which these offenders committed were simple enough for the judge to pardon them or to set them free but he condemned them to everlasting punishment in the fire. Their offences were lies, adultery, derision, abuse, lavishness, etc. All these were great sins in the town of Creator. But we did not take them as sins in my village. As the judge put these offenders to everlasting punishment in the fire in respect of these simple offences, I hastily asked with wonder from the head of the drummers that why these offenders did not engage the barrister to diffend them. But this head of the drummers bursted into a great laughter and then he explained to me that: "We have no barristers, etc. in this town because the judge will never judge the cases with a slight partiality!" This head of the drummers explained to me further that all of the offenders who were put to everlasting punishment in the fire were lawyers, judges, etc. who had committed these offences when they were alives in their respective countries

But when the head of the drummers explained to me like that, Ojo, Alabi and myself became sad at the same moment when we thought of all the sins which we had committed and which were even important more than these simple ones which we heard in this court but which we took quite simple. So we left the court as soon as it was closed for that day. Again, the head of the drummers took us to another place. This place was the residence of the righteous people and there we met all kinds of people who were black, white, and light blue people. They were uncountable in number and all were dancing, singing, eating, drinking, etc. when we met them. The merriments in which we met them were so much that one could not describe them.

But as we stood at a little distance from them, I was so anxious to mingle with them and share from their

happiness but as I started to go to them, I saw that something which was quite invisible prevented me on the
way. It pushed me back to the spot on which the head
of the drummers, Ojo and Alabi stood. Of course when
the head of the drummers saw that I was pushed back
by an invisible thing, he told me that I was a sinner
therefore, I was pushed back by my sins which were
invisible agents. He told me further that a sinner could
never be shared from the happiness, etc. of these righteous
people but the only people who could share from their
mirth were the people without a slight sin. But the head
of the drummers hardly explained to us like that when I
hastily told him that I had never murdered people in my
life. But he hastily replied: "Yes, not only the murderer is
a sinner but also the people who are misanthrope, mis-
advisers, misadventurers, deceivers, debasers, etc. etc.
etc.!"

Then after one hour that we watched these righteous
people with their fascinating merriments, the head of the
drummers told us to follow him and we did so. When
we came out from the residence of these righteous people,
he took us round the town and there we saw that there
was no a single person without great joy. But we were
afraid that whenever we met the people on the road they
would branch to another part of the road at the same time.
They did not want us to meet them on the road. But when
I asked from the head of the drummers that why the
people were running away from us as if we were their
enemies who wanted to kill them. He explained to us that
these people were running away from us just to protect
themselves from sins because we were sinners and they
did not want to become sinners.

This town of the Creator was very beautiful and clean. There were uncountable of mighty buildings from which we heard the people shouting, singing, etc. with great joy. So having gone round some part of the town, the head of the drummers took us back to his own residence when he noticed that we needed some rest. He gave us a separate flat which contained a big sitting room, bedrooms, etc. As soon as we entered the sitting room and we rested for a few minutes, one lady came to us, she told us to go to the dining room. When we went there, we met variety of delicious food and drinks on the long table. Then the three of us, Ojo, Alabi and myself, ate the food to our entire satisfaction. After that we started to enjoy ourselves with the drinks. We could not even finish the drinks when the head of the drummers came in to us and he joined us to drink the drinks as he was discussing with us how to become sinless fellows. But as soon as we finished the drinks by eight o'clock in the night, he went back to his flat and then the three of us went to the bedrooms and we slept with happiness.

By six o'clock in the following morning, we woke up, but as soon as we went to the sitting room and sat down quietly, he came in to us. Having greeted us, he asked us to dress up and follow him and we did so at the same time. Then he took us to a very wide field where the various kinds of beautiful animals which they were riding were kept. They were riding animals in the town of the Creator instead of motor cars. We met more than ten thousand various kinds of beautiful animals in this field. This field was about five miles distance from the residence of the Creator although this town (as called) of the Creator had no an end at all.

When he took us to this field, he told each of us to mount one animal which he preferred most. So I mounted one of the beautiful horses, Ojo mounted one beautiful camel while Alabi mounted one fine zebra, and the head of the drummers himself mounted one beautiful white horse. As soon as the whole of us had mounted the animals, he told the three of us to follow him. Having left this field we travelled for about two hours before we came to one mighty building which was the hotel for that area. Then he came down from his horse and the three of us came down from our animals as well. He told us to let us enter this beautiful hotel. When all of us entered we met more than five hundred people who were eating and drinking at that time.

Without hesitation he told us to sit down and we hardly sat down when various kinds of food and drinks were brought to us by the waiters. So he and the three of us ate as much as we could from the food. After that we enjoyed the drinks for one hour before we left the hotel without paying money for all that we consumed there because everything was free of charge in this town of the Creator. So when every one of us mounted his animal, he told us to follow him and we did so. Having travelled with him for about two hours, we came to one fearful place. This fearful place seemed as if it had no an end. When we went nearer we saw the big flame of fire which rose up to the height of about eight miles and it was thundering so heavily and continuously that it was easily deafened those who went too near it. But we were still about half a mile away when the head of the drummers told us to stop so that we might not be deafened by the thousands of thunderbolts which were shooting high up from the bottom of the big flame like arrows, and the great echo which was roaring heavily so that every part of that place was shaking as if it was going to sink down.

As soon as we stopped he told us to cover our ears with palms so that we might not be deafened by this great noise and he himself covered both his ears with both palms as well. After that he told us to follow him to one long house which was on top of a high hill. This hill was in front of the fearful place where this great fire was. When we entered this house, he told us to take our palms away from our ears. When we did so we heard no noise any more because this house was a noise-proof type. Then he and the three of us sat down on one long seat which we met in the house but we were seeing the big flame well although it was far away from us. As we sat down with him but as Ojo, Alabi and myself were still stretching out the necks just to see who were in the big flame. He stood up, he drew one long flat and thick glass from left and he pushed it across the wide window through which we were looking at the big flame. He told us to be looking at this thick glass. But as soon as we fastened our eyes on it, it was so transparent that we were seeing the whole people who were in this big flame very clearly as if we were with them. The transparency was so much that after a while I began to distinguish a number of the people who had died in my village long ago from the rest uncountable people who were together in this big flame. All were burning repeatedly and thousands of the thunderbolts were dashing on each of them at a time.

Some of the people that I knew before they died in my village and who were in this big flame, were judges who were not honest in judging cases, except when bribery was offered. The murderers, liars, thieves, deceivers, etc. etc., and many politicians who had embezzled the states' money, lands, etc.

When we looked at these suffering people till five o'clock in the evening, then the head of the drummers pushed the glass through which we saw the people in the big flame to one side and we saw them no more. After that he sat in front of us, he lectured us for thirty minutes that when we returned to our village we must be righteous in everything that we were doing and that we must continue to do so till we died otherwise we would go to the big flame. Not knowing that this head of the drummers brought us to this fearful place just to learn a lesson from the sinners. So we thanked him greatly when we understood what he brought us there for. After the lecture he told us let us go and we followed him to the place where we left our animals in the green field. When every one of us mounted his animal, then we went back to his residence. When we came down from the animals and as his servants were returning them to their field, he led us to our flat. Having chatted with us for some minutes, he left for his own. But as soon as he left two beautiful ladies brought food and drinks to us. Having satisfied our hunger and drunk some of the drinks we went to beds.

In the following morning, at seven o'clock, the head of the drummers came in to us, he greeted us cheerfully as he was usually doing every morning. But as he was still chatting with us the breakfast and the drinks were brought to us. So we ate and drank together with him. Having rested for a few minutes he asked us to follow him and we did so. But as he noticed that before he brought us to this town of the Creator the hairs on our heads were grown to such a length that they fell on our eyes and necks, our moustaches were so much that they covered the mouths and our beards were so long that they covered the chests. All of the dresses on our bodies had already been torn into thousand pieces and all were so dirty together with the over-grown hair of our heads, moustaches and beards that the three of us were no better than a barbarian.

So as we followed him he took us directly to the barber who cut all of the hairs on our heads, moustaches and beards as short as possible. Having done that, the head of the drummers took us to another part of the town where there was a large spring of water. Then the attendants that we met there washed us with the sponge and soap and we were now very clean. After that they took us in to a small house which was near there. They gave us new dresses which we wore at the same time. Having done all that, the head of the drummers took us back to his residence and he did not allow us to go out throughout that day again.

In the following morning, at seven o'clock, the head of the drummers who had already dressed up in the usual uniform that which he was wearing before appearing before the Creator, came in to us. He greeted us cheerfully, he sat down and began to chat with us as he was doing with us every morning. As we were still chatting together, two beautiful ladies brought in the delicious food and many kinds of drinks. When we ate and drank to our satisfaction together with the head of the drummers, he stood up, he told us to follow him and we did so.

When we trekked in the town for about twenty minutes we came to the residence of his disciples. They were six in all. All had already dressed up in their uniforms before we arrived there. So without hesitation, they took their drums and then the whole of us followed their master who was the head of the drummers. After a while we came to the residence of the Creator. As soon as the gate-keeper who was in white attire opened the main gate, the whole of us entered. When we were at a distance of about three hundred yards to the throne of the Creator, then the head of the drummers and his six disciples began to beat their drums and they were singing as we were getting nearer to the throne.

When the whole of us walked stately to the distance of one hundred yards to the throne and as the head of the drummers and his disciples were still glorifying the Creator with their drums and song. One holy man came out to us, he spoke gently to the head of the drummers to stop their drums and song. When they stopped, he asked from him: "Who are these three persons?" The head of the drummers explained to him that the three of us were complainants who had come to the Creator for complacency. He told him as well that we had left our town for more than six months. Then the holy man allowed the head of the drummers and his six disciples to enter. He led them to the Creator and we saw them no more except the sound of their drums which we were just hearing faintly. It was like that we were not allowed to enter and see the Creator personally by this holy man.

But thirty minutes later, this holy man came back to us with one big book and one big pen in hand. When he came to us, he stood in front of us, he opened the big book, he first read out all the sins that which each of us had committed. Having read them out to us, he lifted his head up and said: "It is a pity that none of you is qualified to see the Creator personally because of your sins! However, I shall write down now the complaints of each of you and then present it to the Creator!" When this holy man told us like that he moved to the right where Ojo stood. He asked him: "Yes, what is your own complaint?" Ojo explained to him: "My own complaint is that I am the poorest man in my own town. I am a hard working man but my debts were increasing instead. Therefore I wish the Creator to give me the money which I can spend throughout my life time without even working! That is my own complaint which I bring before the Creator!"

So as soon as this holy man wrote Ojo's complaint down in the big book which was in his hand he turned to Alabi. He said: "Yes, what is your own complaint?" Alabi explained with great sorrow: "My own complaint is that I am a real hard working man. I am so strong that I was doing the work in the farm daily. My a day's work was doubled that of any of my colleagues yet I am the poorest man in my village. I got no money to marry a lady like my colleagues but I am in debts instead. Therefore, I wish the Creator to give me more than fifty thousand pounds! And that is my own complaint which I bring to the Creator!"

Then as soon as this holy man wrote Alabi's complaint down, he turned to me. He asked: "Yes, what is your own complaint? Is it all about money as well as the first two men?" But when he asked from me like that I first breathed out heavily and with tears rolling down my cheeks, I first told him my name (Ajaiyi): "You see, my name is Ajaiyi! I am the poorest man in the world! You see, my

own poverty have been inherited from my father and
mother. Both of them had died long ago and left me in
their poverty! I am a hard working man but the more
I work hard the more my poverty is increasing! As I am
growing up it is so my poverty is growing up along with
me! I have been to several towns and villages in order
to get money but I got poverty instead! Furthermore, I
went to the red sea in order to get the money, only my
colleagues with whom I went returned with a lot of money
but I alone returned with poverty. And thus my other
colleagues went to the blue sea, they too returned with
abundants of wealths but I alone returned with abundants
of the poverties! Furthermore, I have been driven away
from my village from quite a long time by poverty! Now,
what I wish the Creator to do for me is to give me several
thousands of pounds so that I may be free from my
poverty!" But when I explained my own grievances to the
holy man. He shook his head with wonder. Then as
soon as he wrote my complaints down in the big book of
his hand, he told us to wait and then he entered the residence of the Creator with the book. Then the three of
us were waiting with the hope that he would soon return
to us with uncountable bags of money.

But we waited and waited for good four days in vain.
He did not return to us or to come out for another purpose
whatsoever. As we were still waiting there although food
and drinks were giving to us regularly by the servants of
this holy man, it was so millions of people from the four
corners of the world were arriving and they met us there.
Everyone of them brought his or her own problems to the
Creator to be solved. But all of their problems were about
money like ours.

But when it was the seventh day that he had left us there, he returned to us but with the same big book instead of money. Immediately he returned he stood in front of us, he opened the big book and then started to read out to us the comments of the Creator concerning our problems: "Now, you should listen to the Creator's comments on your requests. The Creator Almighty said that since the three of you have not asked for the heavenly thing but money. And since the money is the father of all evils and the creator of all insincerities of the world. Therefore, if you don't want something from this town of the Creator which can bring you out of your sins but only money which rules the world. You should go back to your town or village to seek for the Devil, the ruler of the world. He will certainly give you the money that which you require! Please, go to the Devil, the enemy of Truth. He is not in this town! Please, turn your backs to this residence of the Creator and leave here now!"

When this holy man read out to us the Creator's comments on our requests like that and then told us to leave the town immediately. The three of us bursted in tears at the same time. And without hesitation, we left the town of the Creator with the empty hands for our village. But it was not certain whether we would reach the village without being killed in the jungles by the evil spirits, monsters, etc., etc.

Although we enjoyed good food and drinks and we visited many places and we learned many useful lessons but as "a tortoise's shell is a house of the poverty and if the tortoise is taken to the wealthy town, yet it will still be living in its own house of poverty", so we took our poverty back with us. This was a great pity to us.

WE LEFT THE TOWN OF THE
CREATOR WITH EMPTY HANDS

~~~~~~

*A foreign town will never be so attractive
that one would not prefer to go home.*

*

But of course we were returning to our village but
we were carrying our poverty back to the village as
well. Although "a foreign town will never be so attractive that one would not prefer to go back home", but
there was no one who would go to this town of the
Creator would prefer to leave there if he was not forced
to leave. But of course there was nothing like money in
this town of the Creator. All of the inhabitants hated
money as it was the father of all evils and the creator of all
insincerities of the world.

However, the three of us kept going as we were weeping bitterly for our disappointment to get the money
from the Creator as we supposed him to do. Having
trekked till six o'clock in the evening, we came to the
end of the road on which we had been travelling from the
town of the Creator. Then we continued our journey in
the forest. But we could not travel so far in it when
the darkness did not allow us to see again, then we
stopped. And as there was a big rock, we climbed it, we
sat down on top of it. But as it was the dry season,

the moonbeam was so clear that we saw ourselves and the surrounding of that place clearly.

So without fear we began to decide again whether to go to another town probably we could succeed to get the money from there. But as we were still thinking of the next town to go and did not know, Ojo told us that he knew the town of the god of Iron. When he mentioned the name of the god of Iron, we first refused to go there because he (god of Iron) was very tough and cruel and that he might kill us and drink our blood instead to give us the money. However, at last when we did not know any other town to go again, we expelled our fear and we agreed to go to him. But we did not know the exact place that his town was. But as soon as the three of us agreed to start to find where his town was we fell asleep unexpectedly.

In the following morning, it was hardly daybreak when I first woke. But when I saw that there was nothing happened to the three of us, I woke Ojo and Alabi. I told them loudly to stand up and let us continue our journey because we had not yet reached where we were going to and that we had not got the money in respect of which we had left the village from a long time. Having told them boldly like that, they did not hesitate to wake up. Then with our cutlasses, etc. we continued our journey in this forest. Having travelled till twelve o'clock, we came to one monkey-nut tree. We stopped under this tree, Ojo climbed it to the top, he plucked many nuts down. When he came down, we ate these nuts to our satisfaction but there was no any stream near this place from which we could get water to drink.

However, when we rested for about one hour, we

continued our journey in this same forest. But of course we were very lucky that we were not disturbed by any harmful creature for about four months that we were travelling in the thick forests and jungles except the wasps and bees which were stinging us as we were travelling along. Thus we were travelling along until one day when we came to one wide footpath. When we came to this footpath unexpectedly we stopped, we began to think whether to continue our journey on it. At last we decided to be travelling along on it perhaps we might come to a big town at the end of it.

Having rested for a while, we stood up, we began to travel along on it. But when we had travelled about three miles, Ojo understood that it was the road which led to the town of god of Iron. However, we kept going along on it until we travelled for two hours. When we were about to stop to rest, because we were then tired. We came to one strong gate which crossed this road. So without hesitation and with bravery, I knocked at the door of this gate. I knocked at it so heavily that a person who was at a distance of two miles away heard it clearly. I shouted loudly: "Give way for us to pass in, the gate-keeper! Give way, the gate-keeper!" With a fearful voice the gate-keeper shouted greatly: "Yes, the way is clear! But are you versed in mystery or an ignorant person?"

Without hesitation and with bravery, I replied: "The three of us are surely versed in mystery and we are not ignorant persons!" But as I replied boldly like that, this gate-keeper did not believe me. And instead to open the gate for us, he took his long spear. As he was opening the gate just to come to us to pierce us to death with the spear, we appeared in front of him unexpectedly without opening the gate for us. Without hesitation, and with fearless voice, I greeted him: "Good sunrise!" (about ten o'clock in the morning). This god of Iron's gate-keeper was greatly shocked when he saw the three of us in front of him without opening the gate for us. And before he answered to my greeting, I stretched my left hand (this is the hand of mystery) to him and I shook hands with him fearlessly and I spoke to him with a cheerful voice.

As this gate-keeper scowled at us, he asked: "By the way, where are you coming from and where are you going to?" But before I answered to his question, I first winked to Ojo and Alabi to keep calm. Then I explained to him: "We are returning from the town of the Creator but now we wish to see the god of Iron!" With another fearful voice, this giant-like gate-keeper asked again: "What are you going to see the god of Iron for!" Again with bravery, I replied: "Please, the gate-keeper, don't take it as an insult, I cannot tell you what we are going to see the god of Iron for. It is a secret which is best known to us but when we see him with our own eyes, we shall tell him what we come to him for!"

"Then in a friendly words, the gate-keeper explained to us: "Yes, you are right to tell me that what you come to tell my lord, the god of Iron, is a secret which you could not disclose to me. I do not take it as an offence, but before you can see the god of Iron, the greatest hero of all the other gods, the most merciless god who has water in the house but bathes with the blood of man, you will remain at this gate for about ten days. Because the god of Iron is not available at present and he will not be available until ten days. He is now in his smithery shop and he is so busy that he can not attend to even his own followers how much more for visitors like you, who are really his animals!" But when this gate-keeper explained to us like that the three of us were so feared that we were confused at the same moment. We did not know what to do again.

After a while, I told Ojo and Alabi to let us return from this gate to our village because I did not want to loose my life although I was in great poverty. I hardly suggested like that with fear when Alabi asked from the gate-keeper: "Please, gate-keeper, what is your lord, the god of Iron, doing in his smithery shop which will keep him there for ten days? You know, we are in hurry to see him!" Then the gate-keeper replied without hesitation: "Thank you! the god of Iron is preparing for his yearly festival which will be started in five days time and the celebrations of the festival will last for ten days!"

But when this gate-keeper explained to us like that, Ojo told him that we could not wait for ten days at the gate for we wanted to see him (god of Iron) as quickly as possible so that we might return to our village in time. Ojo hardly explained to him like that when he said with great anger: "Well, if you do not believe all I have told you, I don't mind to take you to his deputy. But as soon as the deputy sees the three of you, he will be happy to detain you until the arrival of the god of Iron who will sacrifice you, together with the thousands of other people who had already been captured, to his gods during the time of celebrations of his yearly festival! As you said before that you were in hurry to see the god of Iron because you wanted to return to your village in time. It is not so at all. I am perfectly sure, once the god of Iron has seen you, not you will return to that your village again but your own spectres because he will kill you immediately! Now, I advise the three of you to discuss together whether to return from this gate to your village!"

When this gate-keeper explained further to us like that, we walked to a short distance from him so that he might not hear our discussions. Then we discussed together. Alabi first suggested whether we should follow the advise of the gate-keeper or not. But Ojo hastily objected to his suggestion. He said that we must not follow the gate-keeper's advice at all. When Ojo said so, I asked him that why we should not follow his advice. Then he made it clear to us that he was sure, the gate-keeper was just deceiving us that the god of Iron was busy in his smithery shop and that he would sacrifice us to his gods if we went to him this time he was preparing to celebrate his yearly festival.

When Ojo said that he did not believe the gate-keeper's advice, I said: "I too did not believe the gate-keeper's advice. Probably he knew that if we could get in touch with him (god of Iron) and tell him that we want him to help us to get money he would give us thousands of bags of money. And I am sure, he would not kill us if we meet him, we are not animals. Therefore we should tell the gate-keeper to lead us to him or his deputy and we should not agree to wait at the gate for ten days or to return from the gate to our village as he had told us to do, perhaps he was just decoying us to kill us or to sell us as slaves! Let us go back to him (gate-keeper) now and tell him to take us to the god of Iron or his deputy".

When I told Ojo and Alabi like that, then the three of us went back to the gate-keeper, we told him that we could not wait for ten days at the gate and we could not return from there to our village without seeing the god of Iron, therefore we wanted him to take us to him (god of Iron). It was like that we insisted to see the god of Iron. Without hesitation the gate-keeper took his dart or spear which was more than eleven feet long with many sharp branches of iron on top. Then he began to lead us along on the road to the town of the god of Iron as he pointed his fearful spear to us.

WE ARE NOW IN THE GOD OF
IRON'S TOWN

∽∽∽∽∽∽∽∽∽∽∽∽∽∽∽∽∽∽∽∽∽∽∽∽∽∽∽

There are uncountable skulls at the god of Iron's shrine; but many of the people who were killed were innocent.
(The shrine of the god of Iron was the place of execution of the people who were condemned to death in former days.)
Truths are failed to sell in the market but lies are purchased with high price without pricing it. The rope of the truth is thin but there is nobody who can cut it; the rope of lie is as thick as a large pillar but it can be cut easily into a thousand pieces.

*

As soon as this giant-like gate keeper of the god of Iron led us to the palace of the god of Iron, his master, he took us to the deputy of the god of Iron. He hardly handed us to him when he returned to the gate. Then as we stood before the deputy, he asked from us whether we came there to surrender ourselves to be sacrificed to the god of Iron. But the three of us hardly shook heads and said "no" but we came there just to ask the god of Iron to give us money, when he jumped up from his seat with great anger. He took one of the heavy clubs of iron which were scattered all over the floor. Then without mercy, he beat us for one hour. When he saw that we fell down and fainted, then he told some of his attendants to drag us to one fence. This fence was made of the strong irons by the god of Iron. And there we met more than two thousand captives and also uncountable of animals as dogs, goats, etc. All of them were kept in this fence to be killed for the celebration of the god of Iron's yearly festival and the three of us were now among those who would be killed.

This deputy of the god of Iron was so cantankerous that he had never sent anybody to the fence of iron without beating him nearly to death. But as the fence was near the smithery shop of the god of Iron, we saw him in his workshop as he was very busy. I noticed carefully that he was about ten feet tall and very corpulent. Every part of his body was full of long hairs, his trousers, huge cap, etc. were rough leather of deer. Uncountable of skulls of both animals and human beings were surrounded his smithery shop, the fence of iron in which we were kept ready to be killed, and were also seeing everywhere in the town. The skulls were so common in the god of Iron's town that almost all the roofs of the houses were thatched with the skulls of dogs, birds, all kinds of the animals and of human beings as well. As we were still in this fence of iron, he began to forge one big iron. The iron was so big that twenty strong men could not even lift it up to one inch but the god of Iron simply held it with left hand as if it was a small feather. Then he put it on his large anvil which was about eleven feet square and fourteen feet high.

To my fear, within thirty minutes that he had started to strike this heavy iron as soon as he took it out from the fire, he beat it into the shape of a very big fearful image. There were more than sixty mighty irons in his big hearth and the mighty bellows which was blowing by nine men, was bringing out the powerful flame which was rising above the workshop. This god of Iron was very busy this time in carving the big irons into the shapes of almost all the kinds of the living creatures and that as he was taking out one hot-red iron from the hearth with his long tongs it was so he was taking out another one from the same hearth with bare hand. As he was dashing to one corner of the workshop it was so he was dashing to another, he was examining the images which he had already carved whether they were accurate enough.

There was a big bowl of iron in one corner of his workshop which contained more than forty-four gallons of blood and he was drinking from this blood whenever he was thirsty. Having seen his fearful actions in the workshop, then Ojo, Alabi and myself blamed ourselves for not returning from the gate to our village as the gatekeeper had told us to do. We thought that he was just deceiving us as he told us the truth that if we forced ourselves to see the god of Iron there was no doubt, we must be punished to death especially this time that the god of Iron's yearly festival was near. But of course the three of us believed this day as we were locked up in the fence of iron that "Truths are failed to sell in the market but lies are purchased with high price without pricing it." So as we had doubted the truth of this gate-keeper we found ourselves in the fence of iron at last and we were waiting for our death.

"But of course, the god of Iron had been well known throughout the Yoruba land, in the Western Nigeria. One he who knows the god of Iron will never say: 'Who is he!' otherwise the god of Iron will do a wonderful thing to him which means he will kill him right out. Old people had strong belief that the god of Iron is the protector of the blacksmiths, the supporter of the soldiers, hunters and the ironmongers."

It was like that the god of Iron was busy in carving the images almost of all kinds of the living creatures until it remained one day for his yearly festival to start. Then his bearers carried the whole of these images of iron to his palace as soon as he had closed up. Before he left the workshop to his palace, he bathed with blood instead of water. After that his deputy and many others came, they began to flatter him as he was dressing up in palm-fronds which were entirely soaked with the blood. Having dressed up then the whole of them went to his palace in form of a procession.

In the following morning, before the celebration of his yearly festival started, he ordered all his bearers to go and bring the whole of us from the fence. Having brought us to him and as soon as we stood in front of his palace, he gave one long heavy matchet to each of the bearers who were about two thousand in number. Then he told them to behead the whole of us and pour our blood into the bowls of iron which were put in front of him. Without hesitation his bearers started to behead us without mercy and they were pouring the blood that which was gushing our from the necks of the people that they first beheaded into the bowls. But as the god of Iron sat on his throne it was so he was drinking this blood together with his deputy and the others whose ranks were below that of the deputy. They were singing loudly, dancing, many of them were kicking themselves, many were staggering here and there in the circle, some were jumping high up and falling down headlong and thousands of them were striking the irons very loudly instead to beat the drums. All these were included the enjoyments of the god of Iron's yearly festival.

It was like that the celebrations of the god of Iron's yearly festival started this morning. But as the bearers of the god of Iron were still beheading the captives and as they raised their matchets up to behead us. God was so good, it came to our minds this moment to run in to the circle, to mix up with the dancers and join them to dance perhaps if we did so we might be safe from killing. So, Ojo, Alabi and myself jumped into the circle. Without hesitation we mixed up with the dancers and then we began to dance with them. But unfortunately, the way the three of us were dancing was not conformed with the way and the style they were dancing there, our own dance was quite contrarily to their own.

As soon as they discovered this, the whole of the dancers, etc. stopped and every part of that place became as quiet as a grave-yard suddenly.

As soon as everything became quiet and the dancers, etc. became motionless suddenly but only the three of us were dancing round the circle. Then the god of Iron and his deputy looked up suddenly just to know what had happened to his people but both of them saw us this time as we were still dancing contrarily to the way that his people danced. So without hesitation and with great anger, the god of Iron told three of his bearers who stood at his back to go and bring the three of us nearer to him. Luckily, as the three bearers were taking us along to him, it came to Ojo's mind how his mother was flattering the god of Iron whenever she was worshipping him

when she was alive. Ojo's mother was a god of Iron
worshipper before she died.

Without hesitation, Ojo began to flatter him in his
original family name. When the bearers escorted us to him
and as he listened to Ojo and heard his original family
name from him. He did not know when he stood up
from his throne, he jumped into the circle, he began to
dance with happiness. Then his deputy, etc. dancers,
singers, etc. etc., joined him at the same time. The whole of
us danced with him for more than two hours before he
went back to his throne. When he rested for a while, he
asked the three of us with a cheerful voice to come nearer
to him and we did so with fear. He asked from Ojo: "How
did you know the original name of my family, my good
boy?" Ojo explained to him that his mother, before
she died, was one of his worshippers in the village, so
he heard his original name of his family from her whenever she was sacrificing to him.

When Ojo explained to him like that he shook head
with happiness. At the same time, he told him to flatter
him again. Then as Ojo began to flatter him again, he
and his deputy stood up and began to dance again.
Having danced for a few minutes, he went back to his
throne. Then he told us that we would not be killed
as the rest captives. When he told us like that we were
very happy, but of course the three of us were not
captives, we were finding money about before we came to
his town. So we told him that we were in great poverty and
that we wanted him to give us sufficient money which
could set us free from our poverty. But he replied at the
same time that he was not the possessor of the money but
the Devil. He told us that when we returned to our

village we should go to him and ask him to give us the money. He said further that he was quite sure the Devil would give us as much money as we required.. Having told us like that, he asked us to stay with him to be flattering him until the end of the celebrations of his yearly festival. So as we must not go against his wish, we reluctantly agreed to stay with him.

It was like that the three of us remained with the god of Iron till the end of the celebrations of his yearly festival but we were not happy at all since when he had told us that he was not in possession of money. In the following morning that his yearly festival was ended, we told him that we were leaving for our village that morning. Then he gave each of us one matchet and one heavy lump of raw iron which weighed more than one ton. Then he told one of his bearers to lead us to the gate so that the gate-keeper might not kill us as the thieves of iron. So before we left we reluctantly thanked him and we reluctantly bade him goodbye as well. But when we were about to leave we asked him to tell us what we were going to do with the heavy lumps of the raw iron. He told us that when we carried them to our village, each of us should put his own in one corner of his house and then he should be worshipping it. He explained to us further that one who worshipped this heavy lump of iron meant that he worshipped him.

Then Ojo held the matchet as he put his own lump of iron on head, Alabi did so and I did the same as well. After that we left his town this morning with sorrow as well as we had left the town of the Creator with the empty hands. When the bearer led us to the gate and he introduced us to the gate-keeper, he allowed us to pass peacefully. But we hardly left the gate to the distance of about one mile when we threw the heavy lumps of iron into the bush when we could not carry them further. Each was too heavy for even four men to carry. So we could travel as quickly as we wanted to. It was like that we left the town of the god of Iron without getting money.

WE ESCAPED TO THE COUNTRY OF
THE WITCHES

∞∞∞∞∞∞∞∞∞∞∞∞∞∞∞∞∞∞∞∞∞∞∞∞

The hawk plays with the pigeon
and the pigeon is happy, but not knowing that
it is playing with death.
Difficult to cure like the inherited disease.

*

Now, we could travel as quickly as we wanted to immediately everyone of us had thrown away into the bush the heavy lump of the raw iron which the god of Iron gave to each of us which he told us to be worshipping when we returned to our village. But to our fear and surprise, after three days that we had thrown these heavy lumps of the iron away. As we were still travelling along in this jungle, when it was about one o'clock p.m. we heard the great fearful noises at back suddenly. These noises were just as if thousands of people were shouting together loudly as if a terrible thing happened to them unexpectedly. Again, as we were hearing these terrible noises it was so we were hearing the heavy sounds of the rolling heavy things. The sounds were so heavy that all the ground was shaking as if it was going to sink down together with us.

As soon as we began to hear all these fearful things, we stopped, we looked at back but we saw nothing except the noises and the heavy sounds which were coming nearer

126

and nearer to us as we were hearing them. As these invisible things were coming nearer and nearer to us it was
so they were becoming more terrible. When the three of
us craned at the direction from which these terrible
things were coming to us for several times but we did not
see anything. Then without hesitation and great fear, we
began to run along as fast as our feet could lift us. But to
our surprise, as we were running away for our lives, it
was so the terrible noises and the heavy sounds were
following us along as if they were chasing us to catch.

From these noises and the heavy sounds, we began to
hear again clearly and continuously these fearful warnings:

"Wait and carry us along with you!"

"If you wait, you wait for dangers!"

"But if you don't wait, you don't wait for the money!"

"It is better for you now to carry us along with you!"

"But if you carry us, you carry troubles and misfortunes along to your house!"

"If you don't carry us, you fail to carry good-luck
along to your house!"

"If you don't wait but we catch you by ourselves, your
right arm and left leg will be torn away from your body;
and all will be given to the god of Iron!"

"Better you wait now and carry us along with you!"

"But the better you wait and carry us along to your
house!"

"It is certain that you carry vanity, poverty, troubles,
sickness and uncountable of money along to your house!"

"Better you wait to carry us along with you to your
house now! Wait! Wait! Wait!"

It was like that we were hearing these warnings

continuously with the heavy sounds of the invisible rolling thing and the great terrible noises. Not knowing that the three heavy lumps of the raw iron which the god of Iron gave us to be carried to our village were living evil creatures. Although they were not the day he gave them to us but they became alive and began to make great terrible noises as they were following us as soon as we threw them away when they were too heavy for us to carry.

So as these three lumps of the raw iron were living evil creatures, they wanted us to carry them to our village to be worshipping them. But we continued to run faster than before immediately we were hearing them warning us continuously that "the better you wait and carry them along with us the better we carry as well the vanity, poverty, troubles, sickness and uncountable of money along to your house!" Yet as we did not wait to carry them along with us. These three lumps of the iron were then chasing us fiercely along in the jungle to catch us by all means as they were still making fearful noises, heavy sounds and warnings which were so terrible that a strange whirlwind came suddenly. This whirlwind was so strong that as soon as it began to blow, we were confused, we could not control ourselves again but we were staggering about in the jungle. It nearly rooted out the mighty trees, all the birds which were perched on branches of trees flew away with fear and also all the animals ran out with fear from their hiding places and were scattered all over the jungle.

To our fear again, when we ran to the left all of these animals ran to that place as well as these three heavy lumps of the iron chased us to that place. Without hesitation we ran back to the right perhaps we might be saved. But these uncountable animals did the same thing with us and the three heavy lumps of the iron chased us to that place as well with their horrible noises, etc. As we were still running here and there in this jungle confusedly and with fearfulness it was so we were falling down heavily together with these animals because all the vast hills, the ground and the mighty trees were then shaking as if they were going to sink down.

At last when all our efforts to run to the right or left were failed, and as we saw this time that the heavy lumps of the iron were approaching us nearer. We began to run ahead as fast as we could. But these terrible active lumps of the iron were still chasing us along deeply into the jungle and it was so we were running on and on with great fear till we entered one small country unexpectedly. As soon as we ran to this country unexpectedly, we hid behind a house, we thought that we were safe like "the hawk in the sky which does not realise that the people in the land are seeing it". It was so for us this day which was "The Day of Trouble" (Friday). So as we hid behind that house and were still breathing quickly and audibly because we were entirely tired. These three heavy lumps of the iron rolled on the ground to this country. As they were rolling about with their terrible noises and heavy sounds, they saw us in the corner of the house in which we hid ourselves. As soon as they saw us and were rolling to that corner to catch us. We ran direct to the house which was next to the bush.

And without even knocking at the door we forced the door open and then ran inside. As we ran inside and saw an old woman who was the owner of this house, we hastily engrafted her with fear. But to our fear, we hardly did so when these heavy lumps of the iron rolled into this house as well. As soon as we saw them, we left the old woman, we began to run from one room to the other as they were chasing us to catch. As they were still chasing us about in this house, this old woman had understood that these terrible lumps of the iron were from the god of Iron and that they were living evil spirits. So she hastily ran in to one of the rooms, she brought out one keg of the palm-oil. And as these lumps of the iron were still chasing us here and there she began to chase them. As soon as she met one of them but she hardly poured some of the palm-oil on it when it stopped on the very spot that she met it.

As soon as that one had stopped she continued to chase the rest two. Very soon she met one of the two and she hardly poured some of the palm-oil on that one when it stopped on the same spot. And without hesitation she continued to chase the last one which was still chasing us about. When she met it she hastily poured the oil on it and it stopped at the same moment on the same spot. It was like that these three heavy lumps of the iron became liveless or motionless as soon as this old woman poured the palm-oil on them.

Having stopped them with the palm-oil, she invited the three of us into her sitting room. She told us to sit down and rest because she noticed that we had entirely tired. Even we were unable to speak out any word this time, we were only breathing in and out.

After we had rested for almost one hour, she called out loudly her only son whose name was Ishola, to bring food and water for us. Within a few minutes Ishola

brought the food and water to us. Ishola was about fifteen
years old, he was healthy and smart and very cheerful
to the strangers and his many friends. As soon as we finished with the food, this old woman, who was Ishola's
mother, told us to follow her and we did so. She took us
round the whole of her house first and then to the garden
which was more than one acre. She planted almost every
kind of the edible fruits there. In her house there were
only two entrances, one was in front of the house and this
was the main entrance. The other one was at the back
of the house and this was through to the garden. The garden itself was entirely surrounded by the thick high walls.
There were no windows at all in this house.

As soon as she had shown everything to us, she told us
to push one of the three terrible heavy lumps of the iron,
which had chased us to her house, to under one big tree
which was in the centre of the garden. We were afraid
to touch it but we pushed it to under that tree when she
assured us that all of the three (lumps of the iron) were
no more harmful since she had poured the palm-oil on
them. As soon as we had pushed that one to the foot of
the tree, she told us to push the second one to the entrance which was through to the garden and we did so.
Then after that she told us again to push the third one to
the entrance of the front of the house. Having done
so, she told us to follow her back to the sitting room.

Then as she sat down on one high chair she told the
three of us to sit on one long sofa which was in front of
her. Then she asked gently from us: "From where
were you three of you returning?" Ojo hastily explained:
"When the three of us were returning from the town of
the Creator we branched to the town of the god of Iron.

After we had celebrated his yearly festival with him, we asked him to give us money but he gave us the three terrible lumps of iron instead. He told us to carry them to our village to be worshipping them. He told us as well that as he was not the possessor of money but the Devil therefore we should go to him for the money when we returned to our village. But having carried the three lumps of the iron to a short distance and were too heavy for us to carry further then we threw them away. But since the day we had thrown them away, they started to chase us about to catch until we had escaped to this your country and then to your house for your rescue!"

"Yes, in fact, both the god of Iron and the Creator are not the possessors of the money! You had made great mistake to go to them! Only the Devil is the possessor of the money!" this old woman explained to us briefly. But she hardly explained to us like that when she began to tell us her own story which went thus: "To be frank, I am the Chairwoman of all the witches of this country. I am the most wicked witch. In this country, only witches and wizards are living here. I have four other members who are, Ayinke, the secretary of the witches, Odere, the president of the witches, Awele, the vice-president of the witches, and Abeke, the messenger of the witches! So I am powerful and wicked more than all those I have mentioned to you now. They are coming to my house every midnight to hold meeting with me. Although the three of you are finding money about but you have become the captives. You have already brought yourselves in my trap. You are confined into this house as from this moment till when it is my turn to prepare food for my members! You know, I am a basket weaver and also the

field rat killer. My only son, Ishola, takes all of them
to the market for sale and I buy all my needs from the
money that I realize by selling them (baskets and field
rats). I believe, you will remember that I told you to push
one of the three terrible lumps of the iron to the foot of
a big tree which is in my garden; you have pushed the
second one to the entrance which is through to the
garden and you have pushed the third to the entrance
of the front of the house!

"So if you try to escape through the garden, the
terrible lump of iron which is put there will chase and
catch you. If you try to escape through the entrance of
the front of the house, the lump of the iron which is put
there will chase and catch you as well and if you try to do
the same thing through the entrance to the garden the
one which is put there will catch you as well. Now there
is no chance for you to escape from my house. All the
three lumps of the iron are keeping watch of you!
You know, they are not ordinary lumps of the iron but
they are living evil creatures! So before I will sacrifice
each of you to my witch members, you will be helping me
to clear my garden, to make the baskets to kill the field rats
and to do the house works! I had even killed the only
daughter that I had had in my life for my witch members
a few months ago. And it will be one year's time before it
will be my turn again to kill somebody to my members.
But Ishola, my only son, has not known yet that I am a
witch. My three friends, (she called us friends) that is how
things will go. And I hope you do agree!"

As soon as this old woman, the chairwoman of the
witches whose name was Adeola, had told us her story
and said plainly that she would kill us one by one for her

witch members, she stretched right hand up near her head, she took her old hand woven fan from the rack. This fan was woven from the palmyra palm. Then she began to fan herself continuously as she was expecting what we were going to tell her about all she had told us.

Having heard from her that she was going to kill us for her witch members and she told us again that once we had entered her house we could not escape otherwise the three heavy lumps of the iron would chase and catch us for her. The three of us first took a full heavy breath suddenly. I looked at Ojo's eyes and Ojo looked at Alabi's eyes but Alabi looked at the ground. The three of us were so perplexed this time that we did not know what to do. But after a few minutes I became normal before Ojo and Alabi. Then I asked from this old woman: "Why cannot you stop to kill people?" But she said without hesitation: "Why should I stop it! As you aware that it is 'difficult to cure the inherited disease'. Therefore I am unable to stop killing people or to leave my witchcraft which I had inherited from my mother since my youth!" Then she snubbed at us as if we were goats.

As she was still fanning herself, Ishola, her only son, entered. But as he wanted to sit on the same sofa on which the three of us sat, his witch mother told him to take us to the garden and to show us where we could kill the field rats. Without argument, we followed him to the garden. In this garden he gave one stick to each of us then he showed us where the rats lived in a part of this garden. Then he and the three of us began to hunt for the rats. When the whole of us struggled for about two hours, we found one and then we started to chase it about in the garden to kill. As this rat was dashing here and there we were mistakenly beating ourselves with the sticks instead of the rat. However, having tried all our efforts, we killed it. When we took it to the witch mother, without thanking us, she snatched it from us, she hung it on the rack together with one basket which she had just completed. As soon as she had hung both basket and the rat on the rack, she told Ishola to take them to the market in the following morning for sale. After that she told the three of us to follow Ishola to the kitchen to help him cook some yams which the whole of us would eat that night.

Having cooked the yams, we took it together with the pot to her. After she picked the best ones into her wooden bowl, she poured plenty of palm-oil on them. As she began to eat it she told us to take the rest to the other room and eat it. So Ishola took this pot and the three of us followed him to that room. Then we ate it. When it was about nine o'clock in the night, this wicked witch mother slept in a separate room and Ishola with the three of us slept in the room in which we ate the yams. As soon as we lay down Ojo, Alabi and Ishola fell asleep but I lay down awoke. I was thinking in mind how the three of us could escape before daybreak.

As I was thinking in mind like that the witch mother began to snore so I was sure that she too was fast asleep. Then I woke Ojo and Alabi, I told them with a lower voice to let us escape. But Ojo reminded me that the witch mother had told us that if we tried to escape the terrible heavy lumps of the iron would chase and catch us for her. When he reminded me like that I told him that we should not keep ourselves there for the witch mother to kill us for her witch members but as we were men we must try our best first to escape. Then without hesitation, the three of us took our matchets, we went to the door of the front of the house. I opened the door very gently so that the witch mother might not wake. Then the three of us jumped to the outside and left the door open.

But to our greatest fear was that we hardly went to a short distance from the house when these three terrible heavy lumps of the iron began to roll on the ground with their horrible noises which woke the witch mother at the same time. As soon as she woke up she ran to the door, she was hastily commanding the three lumps of the iron to catch us and then bring us back to her house. Willing or not, when these lumps of the iron obstructed our way and that they were preparing to crush us to death. As soon as we entered and the lumps of the iron returned to their respective places, she slammed the door. After that with anger, she stood before us and then she repeated what she had told us: "I have told you that you have already been caught by my trap! There is no way for you to escape but soon you shall be killed one by one for my witch members! But you should put in minds always that these three terrible heavy lumps of the iron (she pointed hand to them) are keeping watch of you always! All right, go back to the room and sleep! Good-night!" Then she entered her room and slept. So with great fear we too entered the room and we lay down but Ishola did not wake at all till we had escaped and recaptured.

THE WITCH MOTHER TURNED INTO
THE PUPIL OF THE EYES

Hardly in the morning when Adeola, the most wicked and the chairwoman of the witches of this country, woke up and called the three of us to her usual sitting room. She told us to go to the garden to cut plenty of the palm-fronds and bring them to her. She told us that she wanted to start to make some new baskets from them. Before we left for the garden, she then stood up before the dead rat and the basket which were hung on the same rack in this sitting room. Then she called out loudly: "Ishola, will you come out and take this dead rat and the basket to the market for sale now! It is time! And this morning is fine enough! Please make haste to go!"

As soon as she called out like that Ishola answered loudly from the other room: "I am coming, my mother! But I am looking for my hat first!" Then his witch mother shouted: "All right, make haste!" After a while Ishola came out with the hat on head. He walked to the sitting room, he took both the dead rat and the basket from the rack and he asked from his mother as he held them: "How much shall I sell the rat?" His mother paused for a while and then replied: "Yes, sell it for sixpence!" Ishola asked again: "But what of the basket?" "Yes, you can sell that for one shilling but not less than that!" the witch mother said with a sharp voice. Ishola: "All right! Goodbye!" So without hesitation,

Ishola went out with the dead rat and basket and he slammed the door loudly as he left for the market.

When Ishola had left for the market which was at a distance of two miles from the country. Ojo, Alabi and myself went to the garden to cut the palm-fronds. When we cut some and brought them to the witch mother, she told us to start to split them into pieces. Having done that she herself dressed them finely. After that she told us to go and cook some yams. When we were cooking the yams in the kitchen she started to weave the basket from these dressed palm-fronds. As soon as the yams were ready and we took it to her with the pot and as she was taking her own into her usual wooden bowl. Ishola returned from the market with the food-stuff and many other things which he bought from the money that he had sold the dead rat and the basket. Then we ate the rest yams together with him.

It was like that we were doing everyday but the three of us were not happy at all since when we had heard from this wicked witch mother that she was going to kill us one by one for her witch members. One midnight, as I was trying all my best to see that the three of us escaped from this mother. When I noticed that she had slept, I dug a round hole on the part of the wall of the room in which we slept. When I did so, I woke Ojo and Alabi and the three of us passed through this round hole to the outside. But as we were running away in the darkness. Again, the three terrible heavy lumps of the iron rolled out from their respective places and without hesitation they began to chase us with their usual fearful noises. Within a few minutes they overtook us and then they obstructed our way. But we ran back to the house when they were just preparing to crush us to death. As soon as we had entered the house each of them went back to its place at the same time. And when the witch mother had made a mockery of us for some minutes she went back to her room and slept. So with tears, the three of us went back to the room and slept. It was like that we failed in our second attempt to escape from this witch mother. So since when we had failed to escape for the second time, we gave up ourselves to whatever might be our fate in this country of witches and wizards.

One morning, Ishola took one dead rat and one basket to the same market for sale. When he got to the market he exposed the rat and the basket on the table. He sat before the table and he began to shout: "Here is the dead rat for sale! It is big and fat! Come and buy it for a cheap, cheap, price! And here is a fine basket for sale! A very fine and strong basket! Come and buy it for a cheap, cheap, price! It is woven from the best palm-fronds!" But as he was still hawking loudly like that and he was expecting people to come and buy them. A few minutes later, three strange men arrived in the market. They were spirits who lived in a far jungle but Ishola thought that they were ordinary men. They were born by the same father and mother.

AJALA (the first spirit): "Yes, how much do you sell this dead rat!" he held up the dead rat by the tail and then asked loudly for the price of it as the rest two were looking on anxiously.

ISHOLA: "I am selling it for sixpence!" he replied loudly.

FOLA (the second spirit): "Sixpence?" he repeated the price with wonder as he was gazing at Ishola.

ISHOLA: "Yes, it is sixpence!" he confirmed hastily and loudly.

BOLA (the third spirit): "Will you sell it for us for a half-penny?" he provoked him as he squinted at the rat.

ISHOLA: "Please put my rat back on the table and go away! You hopeless thieves who want to buy a half-penny rat! Please go on your away!" he shouted on them with great anger.

AJALA: "By the way, how much did you buy the rat in the bush?" he asked from Ishola as the three of them had now become annoyed and then he (Ajala) threw the dead rat back on the table roughly.

ISHOLA: "Oh, but how much did you sell it for me in the bush?" he scowled at them and shouted disregardly on them.

FOLA: "We are not selling dead rats, poor boy!" he replied angrily.

ISHOLA: "If you are not selling dead rats, I too did not buy this one in the bush but my mother had killed it!" he exchanged words with them angrily.

BOLA: "We are not so poor to sell the dead rats!" he said with a smile.

ISHOLA: "But if the three of you are not thieves of the dead rats, you should have not priced this one beyond what it is really worth like that! I believe, you are thieves of the dead rats!" he shouted on them as he had become angrier.

AJALA: "You poor boy like this, has called us thieves!" he scowled at Ishola and he was pointing hand to his chest and panting it as the three of them had then extremely become annoyed.

ISHOLA: "Yes! I repeat it, the three of you are the thieves of the dead rats!" he confirmed loudly with bravery.

FOLA: "All right, I am going to show you now that the three of us are no ordinary men!" he shouted on Ishola with a very bad temper.

ISHOLA: "If you are not the ordinary men, what are you then? Are you gods or the rulers of the jungle? Tell me now!" he shouted on them as a large number of onlookers had then gathered round them.

Now, without hesitation, as these three spirits had now become extremely annoyed. Bola, who was the third spirit, looked around there and saw a small bush behind. Then he pointed finger to this dead rat and then to the small bush. He began to command loudly: "Oh, let this dead rat become alive and return to this bush now where it came from!" But to Ishola's and the onlookers' surprise, Bola hardly commanded this dead rat when it came alive and without hesitation it began to run back into the bush. And without hesitation, Ishola began to chase it along in the bush to catch. He was scrambling it as he was shouting greatly: "Ah, my rat is running back into the bush!"

But he failed to catch it until it was disappeared into the bush. Then he ran back, he held Bola roughly and began to shout on him greatly: "You must find my rat for me now!"

Then the onlookers began to part them as they were exclaiming loudly with wonder: "Hah, the dead rat has become alive and run back into the bush! This is first of its kind! Ishola, better you run back to your country and tell your mother about these wonderful strange men!" So Ishola left Bola and then he ran back to his country. As soon as he had left these three spirits, Ajala, Bola and Fola, walked to another part of this market and were disappeared suddenly. As soon as they were disappeared the onlookers walked away with wonder and fear.

As Ojo, Alabi, myself and the witch mother were still busy in weaving the basket in the sitting room. And the mother sat on the floor and was singing loudly. Ishola ran in unexpectedly. Immediately he ran in he sat on the chair behind his witch mother and began to breathe in and out audibly as if he had been chased on the way by the kidnappers.

ISHOLA: "Oh, Almighty!" he shouted suddenly to the hearing of everyone of us.

His witch mother and the rest of us were startled. Then the mother stood up suddenly and walked to him. Then she hastily asked:

"What has happened to you, Ishola? Were you chased on the way by the kidnappers?"

ISHOLA: "Not at all! But I have seen wonder in the market today! . . "he explained to his witch mother with throbbing heart.

MOTHER: "Wonder?" she interrupted loudly.

ISHOLA: "Certainly, my mother! And it was the first of the wonder I have ever seen in my life!" he explained as he was perspiring continuously.

MOTHER: "How did it look like?" she asked with wonder as she then bent a little bit forward and paid more attention and listened.

ISHOLA: "It did not look like anything. But . . ." he was greatly confused and murmured.

MOTHER: "And you have seen it?" she interrupted hastily.

142

ISHOLA: "Yes..." he murmured again.

MOTHER: "Hope there is nothing wrong with you in the market today, Ishola?" his witch mother asked with doubt as Ojo, Alabi and myself were looking at him with wonder.

ISHOLA: "There is nothing wrong with me at all but I have seen the wonder in the market today!" he shouted with confusion.

MOTHER: "All right, tell me the wonder which you have seen in the market today!" his witch mother dragged one chair from the left, she sat on it before Ishola and she was then listening to him attentively.

ISHOLA: "You see, my mother, three strange men came to me in the market today. When they priced the dead rat below the price which you have told me to sell it. I called them thieves. But when they became annoyed then they commanded the dead rat to become alive and as soon as it became alive they commanded it again to go back into the bush where it came from. But to my fear, it ran furiously into the bush. I chased it but I failed to catch it. And it was like that the rat was disappeared into the bush!" Ishola explained sadly to his mother.

MOTHER: "So the dead rat has become alive and gone back into the bush?" the witch mother retorted after she had paused for a while with wonder.

ISHOLA: "Certainly! It had gone back into the bush!" he replied sympathetically.

MOTHER: "The dead rat?" she asked with great sorrow as she bent backward a little bit.

ISHOLA: "Yes! I wonder!" he replied after he had kept quiet for a few minutes with wonder.

MOTHER: "So you did not return with any money today?"
she asked.

ISHOLA: "Not at all!" he replied with sorrow.

MOTHER: "By the way, Ishola, did you tell the three
strange men or spirits that your mother is the 'Most
wicked witch of this country'? Did you tell them
as well that I am the Chairwoman of all the witches
of this country?" she asked as she became crazy. She
stood up in wrath and walked slowly to a few yards
and then walked back and then sat back on the
chair as she was murmuring and beating her head:
"Oh, what falls on me today!"

ISHOLA: "Witch! Or what did you call yourself now?
Witch?" he shouted greatly as he was startled
suddenly.

MOTHER: "I am the most powerful witch in this country!"
she confirmed loudly.

ISHOLA: "That means you are a witch?" he gave a sudden
scream as his mother confirmed that she was a witch.
And he stood up suddenly and walked backward to
a short distance from his witch mother with fear.

MOTHER: "Don't you know before this time that I am a
witch? After I change into a bird in the midnight, I
fly to wherever I wish to go but before you wake I
used to return and then I change back to a woman!"
she told the secret of herself to him.

ISHOLA: "That means you are killing people each night
you fly out?" he asked with throbbing heart.

MOTHER: "Certainly! Even I was the very one who had
killed your sister a few months ago, because she
offended me one day," she leaked out another fearful
secret to Ishola with a laughter.

The witch mother turned into the pupil of the eyes

IsHOLA: "My senior sister who was only the daughter
you ever got in your life? Oh, it is now I know that
you were the one who had killed her! Oh, no wonder
she died suddenly like that!" he wondered greatly
and became more startled.

MOTHER: "Yes! I killed her, because she offended me one
day!" she confirmed with a smile.

IsHOLA: "What offence?" he asked sadly.

MOTHER: "One day, she refused to go for an errand and
that pained me so much that I killed her without
mercy!" she coughed and explained to him briefly.

IsHOLA: "That means you will kill me as well very soon!"
he said after he had kept seriously for a few minutes.

MOTHER: But when the witch mother had seen that Ishola
was then so feared that he stood up and wanted
to run away from the house. She hastily stood up, she
went to him and began to caress him as she was
confronting and telling him more of her evil works
which she had done: "My son, do not be afraid. I
am not going to kill you as I had killed your senior
sister. As you know, I have no any other son or
daughter except you alone. Even I am preparing
now to give up my cruel power to my witch members.
Because one day, when I got no money to buy food
and the other things which I required. I changed
myself to one big fine ram with my supernatural
powers. One of my witch members put one rope on
my neck and then she pulled me like a ram to the
market for sale. Having pulled me to the market she
exposed me in the ram-stall for sale. A few minutes
later, one old man bought me as a real ram and the
money that he paid was taken to my house by that

my member. But as soon as this old man had taken me
to his house, he took his knife and started to cut
my neck, for he wanted to kill me for his god. He
cut my neck with that knife for several times, but I
was so lucky that the knife he used was so dull that
it could not cut my neck as quickly as he wanted to.
Then he left me and he went to sharpen it. So he
hardly went away when I hastily changed back to
my former form or an old woman. But this old man
was feared and confused when he returned with the
sharpened knife and met me as an old woman
instead of a ram. Then without hesitation, I was
going away as he was following me along with eyes.
(She bent down and said with a lower voice) My son,
look at my neck, you will see the mark of the knife
which the old man used to cut my neck that day. So
don't be afraid, I am not going to kill you. But don't
tell any of your friends and playmates that your
mother is a witch!" this witch mother explained to
her son, Ishola like that.

ISHOLA: "But I am still afraid of you and there is nothing
which can erase it from my heart that you are not a
witch! You are a wicked witch, my mother!" Ishola
breathed out heavily and shouted with grief.

MOTHER: "Ishola, you should put away from your mind
as from now that I am going to kill you as I had
killed your senior sister! To give you more assurance,
three substitutions are already in the house. They
will be killed in place of you for my witch members
when it is my turn to invite them for party. These
three substitutions are these three fellows (she
pointed hand to Ojo, Alabi and myself). The god of

Iron had provided them for me! Therefore there is
no fear for you at all, I am not going to kill you!
Please take cold water, my son, it will expel your fear
as soon as you drink it!" Then after this witch mother
had convinced her only son, Ishola, in vain like
that, she stood up and ran to the big water-pot
which was at the right corner of this sitting room. She
hastily poured some water into the calabash which
was the cover for the water-pot and then she brought
it to him. But as soon as he drank it he became very
cheerful and had no more fear whatsoever.

But great fear and sorrow filled up our minds immediately the three of us had heard from this mother that
we were the three substitutions who would be sacrificed
to her witch members instead of her son, Ishola. However we gave up ourselves to whatever might be happened
to us in the captivity of this witch mother. So Ishola,
his witch mother and the three of us went back to the
unfinished basket. The mother continued to weave it
while Ishola and the three of us continued to dress the
rough palm-fronds for the mother.

But since when we had failed in all of our attempts to
escape from this wicked witch mother but she was still
confining us for the day that she was going to kill us for her
witch members. I started to pray to the Creator wholeheartedly every minute in both day and night not to let
this witch mother be able to kill us as she was planning to
do.

In the evening, after the basket had been completed
and it was hung on the usual rack in the sitting room.
Ishola took one stick and so did his witch mother from
the same rack near the basket. Then the three of us, with-

out holding anything, followed them to the small bush which was behind the garden. The mother told the three of us to enter this small bush, she and Ishola stood in front of the bush. As both of them raised their sticks high up and got ready to beat the field rat which might run out to death. The mother gave us the sign to start to drive the rats towards them.

It was not so long that we started to drive them when hundreds of them began to dash here and there in the bush. After a while some mistakenly ran out of this bush. Without hesitation both mother and son began to chase them about. At last, the mother tried all her efforts and she killed one. Then the whole of us went back to the sitting room. As Ishola was hanging it near the basket, the mother went to the kitchen, she cooked a nice food and brought it to the sitting room. After we ate, she and Ishola began to sing and dance. As the three of us were looking at them without taking part in their amusements because we were not happy at all. The mother forced us to join them and we reluctantly did so. After we reluctantly sang and danced with them for a few minutes. The mother told us to stop, she went to the doors and closed all. After that she told us to go and sleep in the usual room and she went and slept in her own. That time was about nine o'clock in the night.

As soon as she lay on the mat she shouted from her room to Ishola: "Good-night, my son!"

ISHOLA: "Hope you will not change yourself into a bird and go out to kill people this night?" he asked loudly.

MOTHER: "Not at all! The witches have no meeting this night!" she paused for a while before she replied.

Then she stood up from her mat, she went to the light just to quench it.

ISHOLA: "Please mother, don't quench that light!" he shouted with fear.

MOTHER: "Why, Ishola!" she asked as she was still standing before the light.

ISHOLA: "Because as you are a witch you may change yourself into a bird this midnight and if you do so and come to kill me, I shall see you through the light!" he explained with fear to his mother.

MOTHER: "All right. I leave the light unquenched!" she left the light unquenched but she returned to her room sadly.

ISHOLA: Yet as the light was not quenched, Ishola was unable to sleep for fear perhaps his mother was coming in to kill him. After a few minutes, he stood up, he went to his mother cautiously. He whispered with great fear as he was looking at his sleeping mother: "Oh, I thought she has changed to the bird and gone out to kill the innocent people." Then he went back to the room and slept when he was sure that his witch mother had slept.

MOTHER: "Ishola, get up!" in the morning she first woke up and then entered the room in which we slept together with Ishola. She shouted greatly.

ISHOLA: "Ah, you come in to kill me!" he woke and was startled as he sat up on the mat suddenly. Within that moment he stood up, he ran to the sitting room with great shout. Again, he hastily left the sitting room but he began to run about in the house with fear.

MOTHER: "Oh, my son, I don't want to kill you!" she

149

chased him and caught him as he was just running to the outside. Then she began to caress him.

Ishola: "No! I cannot believe you at all! You want to kill me because you are a witch and you had killed my sister, the only daughter you got in your life! Leave me alone!" he was shouting greatly as his witch mother held him in the sitting room.

Ishola was still shouting greatly when the voices of his mother's witch members were heard as they were knocking at the door heavily: "Good morning here!"

Mother: She hastily left Ishola, she ran to the door and opened it. Then her members entered, all stood in the middle of the sitting room and Ishola was in the circle with sadness while Ojo, Alabi and myself stood in the left corner of the sitting room and were looking at them with fear. We were thinking in minds that moment that perhaps it was this morning they would kill and eat us. Then the mother greeted her members:

"Good morning to you all, my members!"

Odere: "By the way why did you not attend to the meeting last night midnight, you as the Chairwoman of the witches?" Odere, the president of the witches asked with great annoyance.

Mother (Chairwoman): "Well, it was not my fault as I could not attend to the meeting, but . . ." she replied as the other members were listening angrily.

Ayinke (Secretary): "Whose fault it was? Tell us now, whose fault it was?" she interrupted angrily.

Mother: "You see, once I have told my son, Ishola, that I am a witch, he is in great fear that I am going to kill him!" she explained to her members as she was pointing hand to Ishola.

PRESIDENT (Odere): "Your son fears you not to kill him? Is it n't?" she scowled at the mother and then asked loudly. Then all of the four members sat on the long seat which was nearby and after a while the mother sat with them on the same seat while Ishola was still standing sadly before them.

MOTHER: "Yes, Ishola is fearing of not being killed by me!" she explained to the members.

VICE-PRESIDENT (Awele): "Why did you not tell him frankly that all of my own sons and daughters had been killed and their bodies were cooked and eaten by my witch members!" she spoke to the mother sharply and without mercy.

MOTHER: "I have not told him all about that!" she replied as Ojo, Alabi and myself were kept quiet with fear.

VICE-PRESIDENT (turned eyes to Ishola and she explained to him): "Ishola, look at my eyes well. I have killed the whole of my own sons and daughters only on whom I relied and your mother, who is the chairwoman for us, ate from their flesh! So you should not be afraid if your mother is preparing to kill you soon for us! By the way, has your mother told you that she was the one who had killed your senior sister a few months ago and that all of us had enjoyed her body?" the Vice-President of the witches explained as Ojo, Alabi and myself lifted our heads up and fastened the eyes on her with fear.

ABEKE (messenger for the witches): "Ishola, has your mother told you as well that she ate from my only son when I killed him recently for the party?" she scowled at Ishola and asked with a smile.

ISHOLA: "She has not told me that," he replied with a very weak voice as he was trembling with fear.

MOTHER: "I ate from the dead body of her own son when she killed him for us. I even enjoyed it more than my own daughter that I killed last time!" the witch mother or the Chairwoman of the witches hastily stood up and told Ishola loudly.

SECRETARY: "Ishola, let me tell you now that sooner or later it will be your mother's turn again to prepare another special feast for her members and I believe, you are the next son to be killed for her members because she has no any other issue except you!" she interrupted with a sharp and humorous voice as she stared at Ishola.

ISHOLA: "Fear upon fear! This is another fear, my mother!" he stared at his witch mother and said with a trembling voice.

MOTHER: "Never mind and don't be afraid! I am not going to kill you! But these three fellows (she pointed hand to us) will be killed instead!" she walked to him and caressed him.

But when all the members stood up and were ready to leave, the President, who was very stern, stared at Ishola and shouted horribly: "Ishola, look at me well, I am the fear of fears!"

ISHOLA: "So you and my mother are witches!" he asked as he stared at the whole members.

But his witch mother hastily stopped her members as they were about to leave and she told them loudly: "My dear members, this is a good news for all of us!

I have already got three fellows! The three fellows are standing in the corner over there!" she pointed hand to us and her members looked at us for a few minutes as she explained to them further that: "The three fellows were provided by the god of Iron. And I am keeping them ready to be killed for you when it is my turn again to invite all of you for feast!" But the President told her at the same time: "We cannot accept these three fellows from you if you kill them now because they are too lean. You have to be feeding them regularly with the nice food but when they have become very fat we can then accept them when you kill them for us. But it will take you a long time before you will be able to feed them fat!"

Ojo, Alabi and myself were happy when the President of the witches told the mother who was their Chairwoman, that she must feed us fat first before killing us. We thought perhaps before we became fat we would be able to escape from her. Having told the mother to feed us fat first, the Vice-President of the witches said loudly: "Well, the Chairwoman (the witch mother), you are fined for failing to attend to the meeting last night! Good-bye!" the members then left.

As soon as her members had left she told Ishola that he should not mind her members. She promised him that she would not kill him for them. After that she told him to let them sing a song that which would expel his fear. Ojo, Alabi and myself walked to them. We then joined them to sing one song. In fact, as soon as the whole of us sang this song of the witches, Ishola had no more fear again. He was then happy and cheerful to the three of us.

In the following morning, Ishola and his witch

mother took the dead rat and the basket from the rack. Ishola held both and then his mother followed him to the market. Both of them left the doors unclosed because the mother was sure that if Ojo, Alabi and myself attempted to escape the three terrible heavy lumps of the iron would not allow us to do so. The mother followed Ishola to the market this morning so that she might revenge on the three strange men or spirits who had commanded the dead rat to become alive and run back into the bush last market-day. But as soon as we saw that Ishola and his witch mother had left for market. The three of us cut a part of the roof of the house as quickly as possible. We then passed through the part that we cut to the outside. But to our fear again, as we were running away as fast as we could so that we might be far away from this country of the witches and wizards before the witch mother returned from the market.

There we saw unexpectedly that these terrible heavy lumps of the iron were chasing us to catch with their usual fearful noises. As they were chasing us along to catch it was so we too were running along faster than ever. But within a few minutes they reached us and without hesitation they obstructed our way. They did not allow us to move. But as they wanted to crush us to death we returned to the house at the same time. That was our third attempt to escape but we failed entirely. Then the three of us were expecting the witch mother to return from the market whether she would punish us for a part of the roof of her house which we had cut.

When she got to the market with Ishola, they put both basket and the dead rat on the table. Then Ishola began to shout repeatedly: "Here is the basket for sale! It is a nice basket! Here is the dead rat for sale! A very fat rat!" As Ishola was still shouting like that, the three spirits came again. They then began to price both basket and the dead rat:

AJALA (the first spirit): "Yes, how much is your dead rat this morning?" he asked loudly as many people came nearer and surrounded them and were listening as the witch mother stared at the three spirits.

ISHOLA: "My dead rat is one shilling this morning!" he shouted on them disrespectly.

FOLA (the second spirit): "Will you sell it for us for one farthing?" he priced the rat as he held it up by the tail.

ISHOLA: "You come again! I shall sell it for one shilling and there is no reduction!" he replied angrily as his mother scowled at them (the three spirits).

BOLA (the third spirit): "How much is your basket as well?" he interrupted while the mother was looking at them with great anger.

ISHOLA: "My basket is one shilling as well!" he replied as he snubbed at them.

BOLA: "Will you sell it for us for one fathing as well?"

ISHOLA: "Go away from here, the three thieves! Go away!" he shouted on them in such a shameful way that all the people or onlookers who had surrounded them bursted into a great laughter suddenly.

AJALA (the first spirit): "You call us thieves?" he asked quietly as the three of them had become annoyed.

MOTHER: "Yes! The three of you are expert thieves! But if you are not thieves why then did you price both rat and basket so cheaply as if though I had stolen them from the bush! Go away from here!" she

shouted on them with anger and the onlookers
bursted into a great laughter again.

Fola (the second spirit): "All right, as you have called
us thieves, I shall let you see now what you have
not seen in your life before! And . . ." he told the
mother angrily as he scowled at her.

Mother: "By the way, what are you?" she interrupted
suddenly.

Bola (the third spirit): commanded suddenly "Oh, let
this dead rat become alive now and run back
into the bush where it came from and let this
basket become the palm-fronds and go back onto
the palm-tree on which they had been cut!" he
commanded as the rest two were looking on angrily
while Ishola and his witch mother were standing up
with great passion.

Mother: "Come back, rat! And come back, basket!"
she commanded hastily as the rat had become alive
and was running back into the nearby bush. She
hastily commanded the palm-fronds to become the
basket. As soon as the palm-fronds had become the
basket and the rat had become dead and both came
back to her. These three spirits were so surprised
that each of them shook hands with her.

"Very wonderful! But will you follow us to our
dwelling place in the jungle?" the three spirits
shouted greatly with wonder.

But as she followed them then the onlookers were
dispersed with great wonder. But Ishola waited in the
market to sell both the dead rat and the basket before he
returned to the house.

Now the witch mother was following these three

spirits to their dwelling place in the jungle. These spirits were living together with their three children and their very old and weary mother. A few hours later, they came to their house in the jungle. And they put the witch mother in one room. She sat on a nice chair and then she was looking on as she crossed legs while these three spirits went into another room. They then began to discuss together and in their discussions they decided to murder her for she had the supernatural power with which she had competed with them and defeated them in the market. Fortunately, the witch mother overheard in their discussion that they were going to murder her. Having decided to murder her the three of them came back to her in that room.

Ajala and Bola sat down and both began to entertain her as Fola was leaving the room to the outside. A few minutes after, he returned with food, water and drinks. He put all down in front of the mother and then the whole of them began to eat and drink. After they had eaten the whole food and drunk all of the drinks, the basins and the empty kegs were cleared to the other room by Bola and he then returned at the same time. As the three of them sat with her and were then chatting with her, she said suddenly with a smile: "But I wonder, the three of you were entirely failed to defeat me when I competed with you in the market!" But these three spirits were then became more jealous of her supernatural power when she chatted with them like that, although she did not show in her attitudes and behaviour towards them that they had decided to murder her.

As all of them together with the mother were chatting and laughing loudly, Ajala stood up, he walked to the

verandah and he called Bola loudly. He told him to come
and he (Bola) went to him. As he stood before him, he
called Fola again to come and he (Fola) went to him at the
same time. Then the three of them stood in the verandah
and were agreed to murder her in the midnight unfailingly
but the witch mother overheard the time that they were
going to murder her as well.

FOLA (the second spirit): "But are we going to murder her
    with matchet or with what weapon?" he asked and
    then the three of them lifted up their heads. They
    began to think with confusion as how they could be
    able to murder her successfully because they knew
    that she had supernatural powers more than them.

BOLA (the third spirit): "Well, I suggest, when it is time
    to sleep at night, we should give one white cover
    cloth to her with which to cover herself. After that
    we shall tell her to sleep with our weary mother.
    But as soon as she falls asleep then one of us will
    go in and club her to death," he suggested to the
    rest and then all of them were agreed to that sug-
    gestion.

AJALA (the first spirit): "But how we can distinguish her
    from our weary mother as both are going to sleep
    together, so that we may not mistakenly murder
    our own mother instead?" he asked from the rest
    two with fear.

BOLA (the third spirit): "One of us who is going to club
    her to death will be able to distinguish her from our
    weary mother because our mother will cover herself
    with a black cloth. I think this is clear enough?" he
    explained whisperly to the rest two.

1ST AND 2ND SPIRITS: "Yes, that is clear enough." All

glanced at the witch mother but she pretended to be napping at this moment so that they might not suspect her that she was hearing their evil plan.

FOLA (the second spirit): "But who will go and club her to death among us?" he asked confusedly.

BOLA (the third spirit): "I volunteer to do the work," he whispered.

AJALA (the first spirit): "But you must be very careful not to club our weary mother to death instead," he warned him with fear.

BOLA (the second spirit). Then he walked back to the room, he woke the witch mother who had pretended to be sleeping but who had heard their plan "Please wake up! I think you are feeling to sleep now?" he beat her gently on the shoulder. As soon as she stood up he told her to follow him to the other room and she was following him. He took her to their mother's room, he asked her to allow the witch mother to sleep with her and she agreed. Then the witch mother laid down on the same mat with the weary mother of these three spirits. Then Bola went out of this room but after a while he brought one white cover cloth to her. He told her to cover herself with it so that she might not feel the cold of the jungle.

As the witch mother took this white cover cloth from Bola and on his presence she covered herself with it. Then he went out of the room when he was sure that she had covered herself with it and that their weary mother had covered herself with the black cover cloth. A few minutes after, the witch mother, having seen that the weary mother fell asleep, she took her black cloth, she covered herself with it and then covered the weary mother with the white cloth which was given to her. Having done so, she began to snore very loudly as if she had slept deeply.

As soon as she began to snore loudly to the hearing of these three spirits who did not sleep but kept watching the time that she would fall asleep. Without mercy, Bola, the third spirit, took one heavy club from the corner of the house. He entered the room cautiously. He first hesitated but after a while, he was able to distinguish the black cloth from the white one because it was dark. He then with all his power, clubbed the white cloth for several times. He then came out to the rest two.

AJALA (the first spirit): "Have you killed her now?" he whispered.

BOLA (the third spirit): "Yes, I have clubbed her to death rightout!" he said loudly.

FOLA (the second spirit): "Very good! We have seen the end of her now!" he shouted with gladness as the three of them were going to sleep in their room. But they never knew this time that it was not the witch mother Bola had clubbed to death but their own weary mother.

But at five o'clock in the morning, the witch mother woke up first, she dressed up in her own garments. After, she walked to the front of the room of the three spirits. She knocked at the door and then she greeted them loudly and with a cheerful voice: "Good morning to you, the three spirits! I thank you for the warm hospitality you had had on me and I thank you also for the evil plan which you had planned against me! I thank the three of you and also your late weary mother wholeheartedly! Thank you! But I am leaving you for my country this morning!

Good-bye!" she then without hesitation leapt to the outside and she was going away as quickly as she could.

These three spirits hardly believed their ears when they heard the voice of the witch mother when she greeted them. Without hesitation, they jumped down from their beds and ran to their mother's room. Bola who had mistakenly clubbed their mother to death hastily pulled her up. But she was already dead. And with sorrow the rest two shouted: "Oh, Bola had clubbed our mother to death instead of the witch mother." As soon as all of them had discovered that it was their own mother that Bola had clubbed to death. They left the dead mother but they leapt to the outside. They began to chase the witch mother who was then running far away.

WITCH MOTHER: "It is impossible for you to catch me!" she told them loudly when she looked at back and saw them that they were chasing her to catch.

FOLA: "Oh, I command you my magic, let a big river stretch across her way now so that we may meet and catch her!" he hardly commanded his magic when a big river stretched across the witch mother's way and then she stopped.

MOTHER: "Oh, I command you my magic to provide me one canoe and one paddle now!" she hardly commanded like that when her magic provided one canoe and one paddle. Without hesitation, as the three spirits were nearly to grip her at back. She jumped into this canoe, she held the paddle and then she began to paddle the canoe across this river as hastily as she could. But before they ran to that river she had crossed it to the other side. Then she jumped down from the canoe, she continued to run along.

Ajaiyi and his inherited poverty

When they failed to catch her at this river, they hastily commanded their magic to remove it (river). Their magic hardly removed the river when they continued to chase her along. But when they saw that she was so far away from them that she was about to lose to their view. Ajala, the first spirit, hastily commanded his own magic: "Oh, I command you my magic, let a great fire be in her way and to stop her now!" And he hardly commanded like that when a big roaring, angry fire was in her way and it stopped her. But as soon as she was disturbed by this fire she commanded her magic to cause the heavy rain to fall within that moment. Without hesitation a heavy rain came and it quenched this great fire at once. Then she continued to run away for her life as she was shouting and waving hands to them: "Here I am now! You have failed to kill me! Good-bye to you, the three jungle spirits!"

These three spirits became angrier when she made a mockery of them. So they continued to chase her along. They determined to kill her if they could catch her. And they were still chasing her along. But when she was nearly caught by Ajala, the first spirit, she reached her country. As these three spirits were still chasing her here and there in the country and when they were about to grip her. She escaped to one blacksmith's workshop.

MOTHER: "Please, blacksmith, hide me! Please hide me! Please hide me as quickly as possible!" she was begging the blacksmith as she held him for protection.

BLACKSMITH: "Sorry, there is no a place to hide you here!" he hastily left the big iron which he was forging and looked around but there was nowhere to hide her.

MOTHER: "If there is nowhere to hide me! Please, hide me in your eyes! In your eyes! Please make haste!" she said loudly as she was shaking with fear of not being found out and caught by the three spirits.

BLACKSMITH: "What? To hide in my eyes? How can a person hide in a man's eyes? I wonder if that can be possible!" he shouted with wonder as he was shaking his head.

MOTHER: "It is possible! Please, blacksmith, let me hide in your eyes! Make haste!" she begged him with a trembling voice.

BLACKSMITH: "All right, you can hide in my eyes if you can do it!" he pointed finger to both his eyes as he distorted his face.

So without hesitation, this witch mother, with the help of her supernatural powers, she disappeared into the eyes of this blacksmith. She hardly disappeared in his eyes when she appeared as a little round black spot in each of his eyes.

A few minutes after, the three spirits ran to the blacksmith. Then Ajala, the first spirit, asked as all of them were breathing in and out audibly: "Please, blacksmith, have you seen one old woman to pass through here?"

BLACKSMITH: "Not at all!" he then continued to strike the hot-red iron on the anvil.

BOLA: "Well, she has already escaped to an unknown place! Better we return to our jungle now!" he turned face to the rest two and he suggested.

FOLA: "I am very sorry, we have beaten our dear old mother to death instead! But we have failed to revenge on this mother (the witch mother)!" he said with a weak voice and sadness.

AJALA: "All right, let us go back to our jungle!" Then the three of them returned to their jungle with sadness.

As soon as they had left for their jungle, the blacksmith called out loudly: "Mother, will you please come out from my eyes now, the three spirits have gone away!"

MOTHER: "Better you allow me to stay in your eyes permanently because they (eyes) are suitable for me more than any other place even more than my own house!" the witch mother replied at the same time with a sharp voice. The blacksmith then was struggling to pull her out from his eyes. He rubbed the eyes with both hands as he was shouting loudly: "Will you please come out from my eyes at once!"

MOTHER: "Here I shall remain for ever!" she told the blacksmith and that was the last words she spoke.

Then the blacksmith went out of his workshop with sorrow. That was how Adeola, the most wicked witch, had turned into the pupils of the eyes. But of course there were no pupils in the eyes before. The eyes were once quite clear.

Although this witch mother had been turned into the pupils of the eyes. As she was now unable to come back to her house it was so she was unable to kill the three of us for her witch members, but we were still in her custody. Because the three terrible heavy lumps of the iron did not allow us to leave her house. We tried all our best to escape but they would not allow us to do so. Ishola was also happy as his witch mother had turned into the pupils of the eyes, for he was safe, his mother was unable to kill him for her witch members any more. Even all the members had ceased to come to his mother's house since the day she had turned into the pupils of the eyes.

Now, the three of us, the three terrible heavy lumps of the iron and Ishola were occupied the whole of the house. Ishola was very cheerful to us at first. We were playing together as we liked in both house and his mother's garden. His friends were coming to play with us as well. But as there was no more fear for the three of us of being killed by the witch mother yet there was fear for us of not being allowed us to go back to our village by these heavy lumps of the iron. At last, after we had eaten the whole of the mother's goats, sheep, fowls, etc. and there was nothing more in the house for the three of us and Ishola to eat. One day, when the whole of us were nearly starved to death, Ishola became so annoyed that he told us to leave his mother's house as soon as possible. He insisted as well that we should leave his mother's house together with the heavy lumps of the iron which had driven us to his mother.

When Ishola insisted that we should leave his mother's house together with the heavy lumps of the iron. The three of us made a meeting and we agreed to leave in the midnight of the day that he told us to leave. But Ojo asked from him that how we could leave the house together with the three terrible heavy lumps of the iron. He replied at the same time that he would help each of us to put it on his head to carry it away. When he said so, the three of us sighed at a time. We then began to blame ourselves that we had made a great mistake as we branched to the town of the god of Iron when we were returning from the town of the Creator. Although the Creator did not give us money but he referred us to Devil that he was the possessor of the money. I added to our blame as well that although we were returning to our village now with our usual poverty but with another trouble which were these three terrible heavy talking lumps of the iron which the god of the Iron gave us instead of money which we were seeking about. But of course he (god of Iron) referred us to Devil as the possessor of the money as well.

But I hardly despaired like that with great sorrow when Alabi interrupted that it was even shameful to us more than to steal if we carried the talking lumps of the iron back to the village instead of money. We failed to get money which we were seeking about since about four years that we had left the village but we were easily successful to bring the trouble back to the village, Alabi emphasized like that when he thought over all the punishments which we had encountered before we could reach the town of the Creator, the town of the god of Iron and especially when we were in the custody of the witch mother who later turned into the pupils of the eyes.

WE RETURNED TO THE VILLAGE
WITH OUR POVERTY AND THE
TALKING LUMPS OF THE IRON

However, when it was midnight, Ishola woke the three of us, he told us to stand up. When we did so, he told us that we should be preparing to leave his mother's house immediately. Without hesitation, we took our matchets, then he helped each of us to put each of the three terrible heavy lumps of the iron on head. Having done that he pushed us to the outside of his mother's house. As soon as the three of us staggered to the outside, he bade us good-bye and then he slammed the door heavily with great anger. It was like that we carried these three terrible heavy lumps of the iron along with us without our wish. So without hesitation we started to carry them along in the darkness as quickly as we could so that we might be able to leave this country of the witches and wizards far away before the dawn.

When we had travelled about one-eighth of a mile to this country, we were unable to carry them further, because each of them was so heavy that the neck of each of us was bent so much that it was nearly to touch his back. So willing or not we did not know when we threw them on the ground and then without hesitation, we began to run away for our lives. But we hardly threw them down when they started to chase us along in the darkness. As they were chasing us along fiercly with their usual terrible noises it was so we too were running along as fast as we could so that we might be able to lose to their view. But to our surprise and fear, as we were running from them it was so they were getting nearer to us.

As they were getting nearer to us it was so they were rolling on the ground so heavily that all of the mighty trees, hills, ground, etc., were shaking as if they were going to sink down within that moment. And it was so they were warning us very loudly and continuously:

"Wait and carry us along with you!"

"If you wait, you wait for dangers!"

"But if you don't wait, you don't wait for money!"

"It is better for you now to wait and carry us along with you!"

"But if you carry us, you carry troubles, misfortunes, poverty, etc. along to your house!"

"If you don't wait to carry us, you fail to carry good-luck along to your house!"

"If you don't wait but we catch you by ourselves, your right arm and left leg will be torn away from your body; and all will be given to the god of Iron!"

"Better you wait now and carry us along with you!"

"But if you wait and carry us along to your house!"

"It is certain that you carry vanity, poverty, troubles, sickness, and uncountable of money along to your house!"

"Better you wait now to carry us along with you to your house! Wait! Wait! Wait for us, the money seekers!"

It was like that these talking lumps of the iron were

warning us loudly and continuously as they were making fearful noises and were chasing us along fiercely. But when we ran with all our power for about two hours, we were tired. We were so tired that we fell down and we were unable to stand up until they met us there. Without hesitation, when they saw that we were so tired that we could not do anything that time unless we rested for some minutes, they surrounded us and then they were repeating their usual warnings to our hearing.

However, after we rested for one hour, we put them on head and then we continued to carry them along with us. It was like that we were carrying them on and on until we reached the village after the third month that we had left the country of the witches and wizards. We reached the village at about eight o'clock in the morning. But as we were carrying them along in the village to Ojo's and Alabi's house and as we were entirely wetted by the perspiration and as our necks had already bent and were touching our shoulders. The whole people in the village saw us but as we were now strange to them although they recognized us, they gathered together and were following us with wonder. They were also shouting on us as they were following us: "Why the moneys you bring from your journey are nearly to kill you? Why? Are these the lumps of the iron which you carry now are the moneys you bring? Wonderful!" It was like that the whole people of the village were making mockery of us. However, as they were still shouting on us like that, cry with great shame, we reached Ojo's and Alabi's house which was at the extreme end of the village. And without hesitation, we carried these three terrible talking heavy lumps of the iron into the house. Then Ojo threw his own in

one room, Alabi hastily threw his own in one corner
of another room and I hastily threw my own down
in one corner of the third room as well.

THE VILLAGE WIZARD TOOK US TO
DEVIL FOR MONEY

∞∞∞∞∞∞∞∞∞∞∞∞∞∞∞∞∞∞∞∞∞∞∞∞∞∞∞∞∞∞

One who relies on a legacy is on the road to poverty.
No one claims relationship with a poor man;
but when he is rich, everyone becomes his relative.

*

The three of us were now in the village which we had
left for more than six years in respect of the money.
As soon as the whole people of the village followed
us to the house and made a mockery of us, went back to
their houses. Ojo, Alabi and myself entered the sitting
room. The three of us sat on the floor, we were resting
because we were entirely tired for the neck-breaking loads
(the three terrible talking heavy lumps of the iron)
which we had carried back to the village instead of money.
After we had rested to our satisfaction, as the whole
house had become almost dust and was full of refuses
before we arrived. We swept the whole of it although all
the walls were cracked and were nearly to fall down and the
roof which was thatched with leaves by Ojo's and Alabi's
father when he was alive, was nearly blown away by the
breeze.

Immediately we finished sweeping the house, the three
of us went back to the sitting room. We sat down and
then we began to think of our journey which became
to vanity at last. But of course it came to our minds this

time that "One who relies on legacy is on the road to poverty." The three of us believed this proverb this day, because before we set on our journey to the town of the Creator, we had a strong believe that we would return with a lot of wealths and moneys that which would set us free from this our chronic poverty. But instead, we returned home with another trouble. As the three of us were still thinking like that with great sorrow. I interrupted that: "It is certain now that I shall not be free from the poverty which I had inherited from my father and mother before they died!"And Alabi cut in at the same time with sorrow that: "I am quite sure as well that I shall die in poverty soon!"

But as both of us had despaired like that Ojo reminded us that: "If it be that we are going to die in poverty, we have to try our best to see Devil first. Because the Creator, the god of Iron and the wicked witch mother, had told us that Devil is the possessor of the money! Therefore, we must go to him and tell him to give us plenty of moneys!" When Ojo reminded us like that, I asked from him that: "Where does Devil live?" He replied that: "I do not know the exact place that he lives but I know one wizard who will take us to him (Devil)!"

When Ojo had explained to us like that, I was not happy to get money from Devil although I was in great need of it. However Alabi and myself agreed to see Devil for money. After we had finished the discussion of how to meet Devil, then we began to think of how to get food to eat because we had nearly died of hunger this time. To get the food to eat was another great problem to us, because we did not return with even one penny except with our usual poverty, matchets and the three talking lumps of the iron. However, Ojo stood up, he told us that he had known one foodseller before we went on our fruitless journey. He said that he would go to her perhaps she would agree to sell some food-stuffs for us. Ojo explained to us further that although he had owed her a lot of money before we went on our journey.

But to our fear again, Ojo hardly stepped one foot to the outside when one of the three terrible talking heavy lumps of the iron (the very one that he carried to the village) made a horrible shout that: "Please come back and carry me along with you!" This talking lump of the iron hardly shouted horribly like that when it rolled heavily on the ground to the outside. It stopped in front of Ojo as it was still shouting greatly to carry it along with him (Ojo). But as soon as some people began to hear the terrible shout, they rushed to the front of the house and were listening to this talking lump of the iron with great fear. Because it was too strange to them to see that a lump of the iron was talking like a human being but they did not know that the three of them had punished us even more than our poverty in the jungle or before we had carried them to the village.

Now, without hesitation and with great shame, Ojo ran back to the inside of the house as a large number of people had gathered round. But these people were greatly feared when they saw that as Ojo was going back into the house this talking lump of the iron was following him. It did not allow him to leave it at the outside at all. Then with great fear, the people shouted greatly with one voice: "Yay! Ojo, Alabi and Ajaiyi (myself) had brought the monsters to the village!" And then all ran back to their houses at once. Now, as this talking lump of the iron did not allow Ojo to go to the foodseller for our food, it meant we would be starved to death soon.

After about two or three hours later, Alabi stood up, he said that he would go to one foodseller probably that one would sell some food-stuffs for him in credit although he had owed her more than one hundred pounds before we went on our journey. But as he stepped to the out-side of the house, again, the talking lump of the iron which he carried to the village did the same thing. It shouted horribly to come back and carry it along with him to wherever he was going. Then with great shame Alabi ran back into the house as the people were just gathering round. When he ran back into the house the three of us sat in the sitting room. We began to think how we could be able to get the supply of food without going out. But there was no way for us to get the supply of food unless we went out. So we remained in the house for three days without eating anything.

But in the morning of the fourth day that we had not eaten anything and we were then nearly to die of hunger. Ojo told the rest two of us to put his own talking lump of the iron on his head. Then he told us that he was going to one of his old foodsellers to beg her to sell some food-stuffs for him. He explained to us further that although he had owed her some money before we went to the town of the Creator, but he was sure that she would sell some food-stuffs for him because she was kind to him. Then he went out as he carried his talking lump of the iron. It was like that Ojo was carrying his talking lump of the iron along in the village to the foodseller. He car-ried his talking lump of the iron along with him otherwise if he had left it at home it would not allow him to go out or to his foodseller.

Two hours later, he returned with plenty of the food-stuffs. Having put the talking lump of the iron back in the room, he brought the food-stuffs to us in the sitting room. As soon as Alabi and myself had seen that Ojo had brought the food-stuffs, I put my own talking lump of the iron on head with the help of Ojo and Alabi. I then took the pitcher, I went to the river which was not so far from the village. I brought the water with it to the house for our use. And without hesitation, we cooked some of the food-stuffs and we ate it to our satisfaction. Having satisfied our hunger, the three of us did not go out to salute our old friends but we stayed at home and we began to play the native game (warry). Because we were not allowed to go out by these terrible talking heavy lumps of the iron.

But at last when we became tired of staying at home always, each of us put his own talking lump of the iron on head and then we went out. We began to visit our old friends. Unfortunately, as we visited the last friend, we put our talking lumps of the iron down in his parlour and then we began to drink the palm-wine with which he welcomed us. After a while we were so intoxicated by the wine that we did not remember to put our talking lumps of the iron on head before we went to the front of the house just to take some fresh air. But all the people in our friend's house and all people around were nearly to die of fear when these talking lumps of the iron shouted horribly that we should come and carry them along with us to the front of the house.

So without hesitation, all the people of that house

175

drove us away with our talking lumps of the iron at the same time. It was like that we carried them back to the house with great shame. So since that day we stopped to visit our friends and they too were fearing to visit us. Not only our friends feared to visit us but also the whole people in the village. But of course: "No one claims relationship with a poor man; but of course when he is rich, everyone becomes his relative!" It was so the three of us stayed lonely at home with our three terrible talking heavy lumps of the iron which had become our lord· But of course if we were lucky enough to bring money and other wealths to the village instead of these talking lumps of the iron, the whole people of the village would rush to our house to share from them.

But when it was the seventh day that we had arrived in the village. One morning, Ojo, who had told Alabi and myself that he knew one brave wizard who would take us to Devil for money, he told us to let us go to that wizard. Then everyone of us put his own lump of the iron on head. Then we went to the next village in which the wizard lived. We reached this village in the midnight because it was far away. When we came to this village, we saw that there were only two small houses and Ojo took us to the house of this brave wizard. But when he saw these three talking lumps of the iron on our heads he knew what they were at the same time. Then without allowing us to put them down in his house, he took us to the shrine of his gods. He told us to put them down before his gods. The shrine was in the heart of a jungle.

Having put them down before his gods, he sat on a big skull of human being, after that he asked us to sit down on the floor before his gods. After that he asked us what we came to him for. Ojo did not waste time but he replied immediately: "The three of us had wanted to see you since last few days for help!"

WIZARD: "Yes, I will surely help the three of you if it is mainly on this worldly problems. I am a brave wizard. I have no fear to say that I am not created by any God but there is no shame in it to tell everyone who comes to me for help that I am the agent for Devil. I have killed more than ten thousand people since when I have been dealing with Devil and I still hope to kill more than that in my life. I have already rendered entirely useless thousands of people and I still hope to render more than that entirely useless in my life. There are thousands of skulls in my house. Bones of human beings are uncountable in my house and it is so uncountable of ribs of the human beings are no more useful in my shrine. But before a person comes to me he should have a firm decision. Therefore, Ojo, tell me now what exactly you want!" this brave wizard or Devil's agent first introduced himself to us like that. But as a matter of fact, his attitudes, surroundings and shrine proved that all what he had told us were truth.

OJO: "My name is Ojo. I am so poor that my poverty has been driving me about since about ten years. All of my friends are so rich that they have married and have got many children although I work harder than any of them. The three of us who come to you now had visited the Creator, the god of Iron and the Wicked Witch Mother for money, but all of them told us that they were not in possession

M   177

of the money but Devil. For this reason, I come
to you to take me to Devil to give me much money
that which will make me rich, even richer than all
people in my village!" When Ojo had told this
wizard what he wanted, he then prostrated for him
for three times and then sat back.

WIZARD: "Yes, Alabi, tell me now what exactly you
want!" he turned to Alabi and he asked from him
what he came to him for with a huge and fearful voice.

ALABI: "You see, the wizard, I come to you mainly to
take me to Devil. I want Devil to give me much
money which will make me richer than all of my
friends. If possible I want to be the richest man in
my village. Because I am in great poverty since
my father and mother had died. The more I work
hard the more I involve in debts. All of my friends
had married and got many children although I
work harder than any of them yet I get no money
to marry a wife. I get no money to buy clothes like
my lazy friends but I wear rags about! I get no money
to buy food but I buy it in credit. As the three of
us who are before you now were returning from the
town of the Creator, we branched to the town of the
god of Iron. We asked him to give us money but he
gave us the three terrible talking heavy lumps of
the iron to be worshipping instead. And he (god of
Iron) told us that if we wanted money we should
go to Devil. Therefore I come to you to take me to
Devil to give me the money which I will spend
throughout my life time!" Alabi told the wizard
all his difficulties before he prostrated for him for
three times and then he sat back.

WIZARD: "Yes, Ajaiyi, will you tell me now what exactly you want me to do for you!" he then turned eyes to me, he asked from me with his usual huge and fearful voice.

AJAIYI: "My name is Ajaiyi. You see, the wizard, my father and mother were in greatest poverty throughout their lives time. Before both of them died, I had inherited this poverty from them. So my own poverty is a chronic one. Therefore it will be very difficult for me to free from it. Before I left my village, I had pawned myself for money to two pawnbrokers in order to be free from it but all my efforts were not successful. At last, I left the village for abroad in order to get the money. I have been to the town of the Idol Worshipper, the town of fire, the town under the river, the town of the Creator, the town of the god of Iron, the country of the witches and wizards, etc. but I did not get any money from any of these towns. But the god of Iron gave Ojo, Alabi and myself three terrible talking heavy lumps of the iron to be worshipping instead to give us money. He then referred us to Devil. Now I cannot go back to my village without getting the money, so for this reason I come to you to take me to Devil to give me sufficient money which will set me free from my inherited poverty!" I explained to this wizard like that and then I prostrated for him for three times before I sat back on the ground.

WIZARD: "Yes, I see to the complaints of everyone of you that they (complaints) are the worldy ones. But now, I want you to understand that money is the

179

father of all evils and the creator of all sins of this world. So if you really want money by all means or through Devil, my lord, who is the possessor of money and other wealths of this world. The three of you should go back to your village and think well. And you can come back to me after three days to tell me what you think about it."

When the Wizard told us to go back to the village to think well whether we really wanted money by all means, we did not understand what he meant by that. But we told him at the same time that we really wanted money by all means.

WIZARD: "Thank you. Now I know that you want money by all means and you shall get it. But you should go back to your village and buy ten white cocks, ten white hens, ten white ducks, ten white drakes, ten white rams, ten white she-goats, ten white he-goats and ten yards of white cloth. When everyone of you have bought all these things then you should bring them to me. But everyone of you must put in mind that his sister or brother will certainly die as soon as you start to get the money. Again, your life will be shortened to six years instead of the remaining sixty-six. But it is quite sure that you will enjoy everything to your entire satisfaction if you can bring all these things! All right, you can go back to your village now with your talking lumps of the iron which are another burdens for you but they (talking lumps of the iron) will be taken away from you the night that I will take you to Devil. Do not come back to me in the daylight but in the dead-night! Good-bye, my boys!" When this wizard

had told us what to do, he stood up and then everyone of us put his own talking lump of the iron on
head and then we went back to the village as he
went back to his house.

But I was afraid when this Wizard told us that our
sisters or brothers would certainly die as soon as we
had started to get the money. I thought in mind that I
was not sure yet whether I would be free from my
poverty until I would die because I would never surrender
my only sister, Aina, to Devil to kill her in order to get
money. I preferred to remain in my poverty rather than
to find the money with the life of my only sister.

As soon as the three of us had returned to the village,
we put our talking lumps of the iron in the rooms as
usual. After, we went to the sitting room. As we sat down
we began to think how to get all the things which the
Wizard had told us to bring to him in three days' time
before he would take us to Devil. But as we got no money
to buy all these things, Ojo suggested that we should
go out in the dead-night and steal them. Alabi agreed to
his suggestion but I against it. Instead, I reminded the
two of them of our sisters or brothers whose lives the
Wizard said that should be spared before we could get the
money.

I told them that I could not spare the life of my only
sister whom I got and on whom I put all my hopes
whenever I returned to my own village. But Ojo and
Alabi said that they were ready to spare the lives of their
two sisters although they had no wives or sons who
were the right persons to be spared for Devil. However,
when it was dead-night and all the people in the village
had slept deeply. Both of them woke me, they told me to

let us go out and steal all the things. But I refused to follow them. I told them that I was not interested in their evil plan. Without hesitation, each of them put his talking lump of the iron on head and then both went out cautiously.

Two hours later, they returned with all the things (ten white cocks, ten white hens, ten white ducks, ten white drakes, ten white rams, ten white she-goats, ten white he-goats and ten yards of white cloth). They kept them in the back-yard ready to be taken to the Wizard. In the dead-night of the third day, everyone of us put his talking lump of the iron on head and then we left the village in the darkness with all these things for the Wizard. We met him in his shrine for he had been waiting for us. When Ojo and Alabi put all these things down before him, he praised them greatly. But when he asked me that why I did not bring my own. I told him at the same time that I could not spare the life of my sister in respect of money. He was greatly annoyed when he heard so from me. But he turned to Ojo and Alabi immediately and said that it was quite sure now that they wanted money by all means and that they would certainly get it. But he reminded them about the shortage of their lives which would be cut down from sixty-six years to six years. He hardly reminded them like that when Ojo and Alabi prostrated before him and made a very strong vow that they would never give up their wishes in respect of the shortage of their lives. He then thanked them for their bravery.

Then without wasting time, he told everyone of us to put his talking lump of the iron back on his head. Having putting it on head, he told Ojo and Alabi to put all of the things which they brought on their shoulders. Having done so, he then told the three of us to follow him without talking to each other and he warned us as well that we must not talk to him. Then we began to follow him as he was going deeply in the jungle.

When we followed him to a distance of about two miles in the darkness we came to a valley. This valley was so deep that it seemed it had no bottom. But what we saw as bottom of it was a mighty fire, the flame of which was rising up nearly to half a mile into the sky. The width of this valley was more than one mile. When we came to this valley of fire, this Wizard immediately whistled loudly and then there we saw a very big unicorn which was coming out from the fire of this valley. With its one long, twisted horn in the middle of its forehead, it was running up towards the Wizard. The three of us were about to cry out with fear but we became calm when we remembered that this Wizard had warned us seriously before we left his shrine that we must not talk at all.

When this fearful unicorn came out from the valley with the fire all over its body, it stopped in front of the Wizard as it started to gloat at Ojo, Alabi and myself. As soon as it stopped in front of him, he mounted it and then he made a sign to us with hand to mount it behind him. With great fear the three of us did so and then it carried the whole of us across this valley of fire. And it hardly carried us to the other side of the valley when it dropped us down suddenly by itself and then hastily went back into the valley and very soon it disappeared in the fire. Again, we were following this Wizard as he was still going deeply into this jungle in the darkness.

After a while we came to a mountain. This mountain was very high but we climbed it to the top within a few minutes. The top of it was flat. And within a few minutes we walked to one circle. This circle was about one thousand yards circumference. It was very clean and lovely to see. As soon as we came to this circle, the Wizard warned us with hand instead to talk, that we must not enter this clean circle, so the three of us stood at outside of it with our talking lumps of the iron on head. As he walked slowly to one-quarter of this circle he stopped and then he started to recite incantation very loudly.

As soon as he started to incantate, feathers and long hairs started to come out of his body. Within a few seconds he was entirely covered with the hairs and feathers so much that the whole of him was just like a round log of wood except his eyes which were then seeing faintly. As he was still incantating loudly and as soon as he began to shiver, he turned to a lion, from that to a very big crocodile, from that to a fearful bull with two long horns on head, from that to a snail which was as big as a house, from that to an ostrich, from that to a boa-constrictor and as it came nearer to us it pretended to swallow us, from that to a very beautiful lady, from that to a boar, from that to a bull-dog and barked loudly at three of us for a few seconds, and from that to an egg which was as big as a round hill and out of this egg there came out suddenly one big cock which began to crow loudly and repeatedly.

As this cock was still crowing loudly, five minutes later there came the thick smoke and then it was spread all over the circle. As soon as the smoke disappeared there we saw a huge fearful man who stood in the middle of the circle and the Wizard stood in front of him. This fearful huge man was in black garments, black slippers, black cap, black bracelets on both wrists and ankles, all of him was as black as black paint. His disciples were about fifty all were in black dresses and all lined up at his back but a little distance from him. Each of them (disciples) hung a very huge bag on left shoulder and held one long spear with left hand as he was in readiness to discharge his duty to his master immediately he was asked to do something.

Ojo, Alabi and myself were extremely feared when we saw all these fearful things but the previous warning of the Wizard hastily kept us calm when we were about to cry and run away for our lives. This fearful huge man was Devil who was going to give us the money. Within a few seconds that he stood astride in the middle of the circle, one man (another one of his disciples) came from the darkness. He walked into the circle, he stood on the right. This disciple was his Augur and he held one big short round bell with left hand and held one short iron rod with the right hand. This big short round bell which he held with left hand was Devil's bell of augury. His (Devil's) Augur hardly stood on the right when another man (another one of his disciples) led one black horse to the circle with a long horse-whip in the right hand. The horse drew one big cart to the circle. Without hesitation, the man opened the door of the cart, he brought out one big table and he put it in front of the Devil. After, he took out one big book and one long pen, he put both on that table. Having done so, he led the black horse out of the circle at the same time. This big book contained the names of his followers and the names of the new members were also writing in it each night that they came to him for money and many other matters.

As soon as the big book was put on the table before

185

him, his Augur struck the bell of augury with the iron rod so suddenly and loudly that even the mighty hills, etc. shook with great fear. As soon as he rang the bell, all of his disciples bowed down and prayed: "Oh Devil, our earthly father, we thank thee for helping us to kill all those we hated to kill. We thank thee also for giving us our daily bread which is the blood of all those died through all kinds of the accidents which thee had brought to them!"

"Oh Devil, our earthly father let us have more blood of the people to drink so that we may not be thirsty any time! Amen!" Having prayed like that the Augur then rang the bell of augury for three times as all of them together with Devil and the Wizard stood in attention and kept quiet. The Wizard led this short prayer.

As soon as the bell of augury was rung for the third time, Devil started to introduce himself to the new members as follows:

"My name is Devil!

The possessor of money and all of the wordly wealths!

The enemy of God!

The friend of fighters, thieves, quarrelsome people!

The friend of idol worshippers!

The friend of murderers!

The enemy of righteous people!

The enemy of God worshippers!

The friend of rascal boys and girls!"

As soon as Devil had introduced himself to all the new members, the Wizard introduced them (new members) one by one to him (Devil) in return. After that he began to mention their names one by one to him and he wrote all the names in the big book which was on the table before him. This Wizard also mentioned the name of Ojo, Alabi and my own name to him as well and he also wrote them in that big book. When all new members had been enrolled, the Wizard asked us to enter the circle and stand at a little distance from Devil. Then each of the new members was asked by the Wizard to put all of the things (ten white cocks, ten white hens, ten white ducks, ten white drakes, ten white rams, ten white she-goats, ten white he-goats and ten yards of white cloth) which he brought, in front of Devil. And everyone did so as quickly as possible with great fear. But when it was my own turn to put all these things in front of Devil, I had none. Then I was immediately driven out of the circle and my name was cancelled in the big book by Devil at the same time. This meant I was not qualified as a member.

After all of the qualified new members had put all these things before Devil, he welcomed everyone of them warmly. Having welcomed the whole of them, he gave each of them one small covered calabash. This calabash was wrapped with black leather and he told him to swallow it. And each of these new members swallowed it at the same time. As soon as each of them had swallowed this small covered calabash, he had the wonderful powers. He could perform any miracle, he could fly to any place, he could change to any form, he could kill any person without going near him or her, etc. He could travel to ten thousand miles and return within a few seconds, he could change a healthy person to a sick person, etc.

After all of these new members had attained the powers to do anything in this world immediately each of them had swallowed the small calabash. The Wizard taught them how each of them would make the vows which he would keep throughout his life time or until when he would come and live with Devil after his death. Having taught them the vows which they would make, the whole of them then knelt down before Devil and said:

"As from this midnight I promise to follow and serve thee (Devil). I promise to depart from serving God, the Almighty. I promise to be unmerciful to those are not Devil's followers. I promise to cause accidents to people so that thee (Devil) may get the blood to drink always. I promise to come back to thee and be thy servant after my death. And I promise to serve with thee whatever punishment God Almighty may give thee in the judgment day!"

After each of them had promised like that Devil then started to ask them as follows:

DEVIL: "Your name is Ojo."

OJO: "Yes, my Lord."

DEVIL: "Are you ready to be cruel to those people who are not my followers?"

OJO: "Yes, my Lord. I am ready to do so."

DEVIL: "Do you know that you are coming back to me after your death to serve your punishment?"

OJO: "Yes, my Lord."

DEVIL: "All right. But you come to me for money. How much do you want me to give you?"

OJO: "My Lord. I shall be grateful if thee can give me up to two hundred thousand pounds! Your worship!"

DEVIL: "Are you ready to spare the life of your sister for me?"

OJO: "Yes, my Lord!"

188

DEVIL: "All right, your wish is granted as from this midnight. I have taken all of your burdens including your talking heavy lump of the iron which is also a burden for you, as from this midnight, but your live will be shortened to six years instead of sixty-six years."

OJO: "Yes, my Lord."

DEVIL: "Do you agree to take back from me all your burdens which I am going to take away from you now when you come back to me after your death?"

OJO: "Yes, my Lord. I am prepared to take them back from you after my death!"

DEVIL: "All right. You can go now, your wish is already granted."

It was like that Devil asked these questions from each of the new members. And lastly he asked the same questions from Alabi. When Alabi agreed to all, Devil granted his wish which was four hundred thousand pounds and many other earthly things. And he also agreed for Devil to shorten his life to six years from sixty-six years. He agreed as well to spare the life of his sister for Devil. Because he and Ojo had two sisters who were left with them after their father and mother died. Then Devil took all of his burdens and the talking lump of the iron from him.

When all the new members' wishes had been granted and their burdens were taken from them, the Augur rang the bell of augury for three times. Then they sang and danced with Devil and the Wizard for some minutes before he (Devil) was disappeared together with his fifty servants and those things which the new members brought to him.

After that Ojo, Alabi and I followed the Wizard back to his village. Having followed him there, he went to his house as the three of us continued to go to our village. But as we were going along on the road, I begged Ojo to help me to carry my talking lump of the iron to a short distance and he refused entirely to help me carry it and Alabi also refused to help me. They said that they were no more in burden. It was like that Devil had taken away their own lumps of the iron but left my own to me to be carrying it about. But I preferred to be in the burden of this talking lump of the iron rather than to spare the life of my sister to Devil and to be his follower in respect of money. Although Ojo and Alabi were now very happy because their talking lumps of the iron had been taken from them and that they were going to get thousands of pounds in a few days' time but their two innocent sisters were going to die soon in respect of them.

At eight o'clock in the morning, the three of us came to the village. As soon as we entered the house, I put my burden which was the talking lump of the iron, in the room. It was like that I alone brought my usual poverty and the talking lump of the iron back to the village.

Now the three of us had returned to the village. Alabi and Ojo could now go to everywhere in the village and other places as they liked, because their burdens or the talking heavy lumps of the iron which had been keeping them in the house, had been taken from them by Devil. And both of them were waiting for their thousands of pounds which Devil, who had now become their creator, would send to them. But I could not go out without carrying my talking lump of the iron along with me. Although they were free to go out to buy the food-stuffs in credit but they were not happy as I was eating from it. They were telling me whenever I was eating with them that: "You have refused to be Devil's son but the two of us have agreed to be his sons and you will be surprised when, in a few days' time, that the two of us become the richest men in this village!"

In fact, within two months that the three of us had returned to the village. One midnight, something which was not visible had brought many thousands of bags of money to the house. Each of the bags contained more than ten thousand pounds. All of the rooms, verandah, sitting room, compound, etc. were full of bags of money. It was even hardly for the three of us before we came out from the room in which we slept when we woke in the morning. Then without hesitation, the two of them re-arranged the bags of money but it was hardly for the house to contain them (bags of money). But I did not help them to re-arrange the money because I did not want to touch what had come from Devil. Now, Ojo and Alabi had become the richest young men in the village.

As soon as the money had been re-arranged, Ojo took one bag, he loosened it, he took about two hundred one pound notes. Having put this bag back among the rest, he went out. He paid all their debts before he came back. When he came back, he and Alabi went to the compound, they held a meeting together and they agreed that the first thing that they would do was to demolish their house and rebuild it even to an upstair. And after that they would marry beautiful ladies. The following morning, they invited the house-builder who would build a very beautiful upstair for them and they paid him his workmanship at the same time. Before the builder left he promised that in five days time he would start the work. But before that day was reached, Ojo and Alabi had buried all the money in the ground except those which they would be spending before completion of their house.

As soon as they had buried their money and were sure that it was safe. Then they removed to one hut which was not far from the spot that their money was buried and I followed them with my talking lump of the iron to that hut. There the three of us were living as the work of their new upstair was in progress. But Ojo and Alabi hated me this time, they did not want me to live or eat with them any more.

But it was a great sorrow to them that when their upstair was getting to its completion, their two sisters, the lives of whom they had spared for Devil, died suddenly. Their sudden death was a great shock to all of the people of this village because they did not know that their brothers (Ojo and Alabi) had already spared their (two sisters') lives to Devil who had made them the richest young men in the village. Although Ojo and Alabi were now rich but the death of their two sisters was a great sorrow to them. They shrank with fear especially when it came to their minds that they had agreed for Devil to shorten their lives to six years instead of their remaining sixty-six years to live. And they became extremely sad too when they remembered many more vows which they had made to Devil before he gave them money. They were sure now that they had made great mistakes for all the promises which they had made to Devil would certainly come upon them soon.

However, when I saw that my poverty was becoming worse than ever, the burdens which the talking heavy lump of the iron were too much for me to bear and that I had no good clothes to wear except dirty rags. One morning, I made up my mind that instead to return to my village with my poverty and the talking lump of the iron. I would leave for another place perhaps I might get money. As soon as I thought like that within myself, I put my talking lump of the iron on head, I wore the only rags that I had, I took my matchet and then I bade Ojo and Alabi good-bye. Thus I left their village for another place probably I would get money there.

But of course before I left Ojo's and Alabi's village thousands of people had become friends with them because they were getting financial supports from them. Although "No one claims relationship with a poor man, but when he is rich, everyone becomes his relative."

I BECAME SERVANT TO THE
DEVIL-DOCTOR

∞∞∞∞∞∞∞∞∞∞∞∞∞∞∞∞∞∞∞∞∞∞∞∞∞∞∞∞∞∞∞

A born and die baby makes the doctor a liar.
One who is righteous will never follow the satan.

*

Although I left Ojo's and Alabi's village with my
poverty, with my talking heavy lump of the iron, which
was another burden to me, with the dirty rags on my
body and without even half a penny in my hand. But
I did not know which was the next village or town
to go. However, as I was carrying along on the road to
the east the talking lump of the iron, which the god of
Iron had given to each of us (Ojo, Alabi and myself)
when we visited him on our way returning from the
town of the Creator. I met one middle aged man on
this road, I greeted him with a tired voice. He stopped
and answered to my greeting with a cheerful voice.
Then I threw the talking lump of the iron down in
front of him. I asked from him whether the road on which
I was travelling to the east led to a town or village. As
he stared with fear at the talking lump of the iron, he
replied that the road led to a town but that town was
still far away.

When this middle aged man told me so, I asked from
him whether I could reach that town before night-

fall. He replied at the same time that it was impossible for a person to trek to the town in one day but two days. After that I asked him again whether I could get a sort of job there to do in order to get money. He replied without hesitation that he could not say whether there was a job which could fetch a man money because he was not a native of the town. He told me further that although the town was very big but the land which was surrounded it was very barren therefore almost all of the inhabitants were very poor.

When I heard like that from him I groaned and I asked him again whether he knew somebody there with whom I could lodge with this my talking lump of the iron. He replied at the same time as he lifted up his head that he knew one middle aged man there who was the only strong Devil-doctor. He told me that I should ask for him as soon as I was just entering the town. But when I told him that I did not like to lodge with the Devil-doctor for I hated the satanic ideas. This middle aged man was so kind that he explained to me that only the Devil-doctor like that one could safe me from the talking heavy lump of the iron. I was very happy when he told me that the Devil-doctor of that town would safe me from the talking lump of the iron. And I thought in mind that it was better to give what was for devil to devil. Having thought so, without asking this middle aged man any more question, I asked him to help me put the talking lump of the iron back on to my head. When he helped me put it on the head, I thanked him greatly and then I continued to travel along on that road and he too went on his own way.

Having travelled till nightfall, I put the talking lump

195

of the iron down, I collected some fruits and I ate them before I laid down and then slept. In the morning, I woke but without eating anything, I tried all my best and put the talking lump of the iron on my head. Then I continued my journey on this road. But I could not travel as fast as I wanted to because this talking lump of the iron was so heavy for me to carry that it was hardly for me to travel one mile before I put it down and rested for some minutes. I was so delayed on the way by this terrible lump of the iron that it was nearly nightfall before I reached this town.

As soon as I entered the town and as that middle aged man had told me. I began to ask for the house of the Devil-doctor, the only person who was brave enough to allow my talking iron and myself to stay in his house. For everybody who saw me with this talking lump of the iron was afraid. However when I asked from the third man that I first met in this town, he was kind enough to take me to his house. But he was greatly shocked when I entered his house and he saw the talking lump of the iron on my head. Because he understood that it belonged to the god of the Iron and that in it (talking lump of the iron) there was a terrible and merciless spirit who was also calamitous.

As it was still on my head and as I stood in front of him, he hastily asked from me: "How did you come about this talking lump of the iron?" I explained to him that the god of the Iron gave it to me to be worshipping it in my village and so he gave one to Ojo and one to Alabi when we went to his town a few years ago although Devil had taken Ojo's and Alabi's own the very night that both of them had become his followers. But as I had refused

196

to be one of his followers, he did not take my own from me, but it was giving me much terrible burdens since when he (god of the Iron) had given it to me although Ojo and Alabi had been free from the burdens of their own.

This brave Devil-doctor then asked again: "Why did you not take it to your village then but to my house?" I explained to him with very weak voice as a large quantity of perspiration was rushing on to the floor from my body in respect of the heaviness of the talking lump of the iron which was on my head: "You see, the Devil-doctor, it would be certainly shameful to me to return to my village with this talking lump of the iron instead of money. I left my village years ago for abroad in order to get the money so that I might be free from my inherited poverty which has now become a chronic one."

Again, he asked from me: "What help do you want from me then?" I replied that I wanted him to help me to get some sort of job to do so that I might get a considerable amount of money to take back to my village. I begged him as well to take this talking lump of the iron from me so that I might be free from its burdens as well as Ojo and Alabi had been free from their own. But he told me that it was a great petulance to Devil when one had refused to be his follower. He told me further that Devil hated such a petulant person so much that he would leave him to his burdens. Having explained to me like that he told me to follow him to the grove in which his shrine was.

When I followed him to the grove, he told me to throw this talking lump of the iron down at the foot of one mighty tree which was near the entrance of his shrine. When I threw it down he hastily poured a kind of oil on it as he gaped and incantated for a while. But to my surprise and fear was that as he poured a kind of oil and then incantated on this talking lump of the iron, I saw that the figure of a living creature (spirit) came out of it in form of thick smoke and within one second it disappeared in that grove. When he was sure that the bad spirit of this iron had gone out of it. He told me that he had driven the bad spirit which was giving me burdens out. Then I prostrated and thanked him greatly for he had saved me from this terrible talking heavy lump of the iron.

But as soon as I stood up from prostration, he told me that he required one servant and that he would take me as his servant as from that day. He promised me that he would be paying me some amount of money every month and that he would be feeding me regularly. He promised me as well that he would give me one wonderful thing whenever I was ready to go back to my village. But he remarked seriously that if I offended him he would call the bad spirit of the heavy lump of the iron back into it and then he would tell me to carry it away from his house even from that town. When he told me like that I promised him that I would try my best to satisfy him in all respects. I made this promise simply because he had saved me from the talking lump of the iron but I had forgotten that things might change in future and that promise was a debt.

Having agreed to be his servant, he asked me to follow him to his shrine and I did so. He told me to take away all the dirty rags of my body. When I took all away from my body, he took them from me, he hung them in one corner of the shrine. After, he gave me new clothes and I wore them at the same time. After that he took me back to his house. When I rested for a while, he told his wife to give me food. Having eaten to my satisfaction, he told one man to take me to another house. This house belonged to his late father and there I would be sleeping because he was so powerful in the satanic work that there was nobody who could sleep with him in his own house. There were many rooms in his late father's house. It was very big with a very large compound. About fifty of his families were living in this house. One big room was given to me to be sleeping in it.

Although this Devil-doctor was a strong gentile but he was very genial to neither his people nor strangers. His shrine was full of people in both day and night to help them solve their problems and to make medicines for them or to help them kill their enemies with his satanic power. He had many wives. The youngest was very beautiful, smart and was cheerful always. But this youngest wife hated him because she did not like to marry such an old man as this. But she was forced to marry to him by her parents and she did so for she must not go against her parents' wish. It was this youngest wife who was giving me food whenever I was hungry.

Now as I had become a servant to this Devil-doctor, he was sending me to wherever he liked. I was following him to the bush or forest to help him to carry herbs with which he made medicines and he was sending me to the market every five days to buy materials for sacrifices. Thus I was serving this Devil-doctor everyday for three months without paying me any money although he had promised that he would be paying me some money every month. One morning, I reminded him that he had not paid any money to me since when I had been serving him. But he explained to me that he would not be able to pay me monthly but yearly. But when he explained to me like that I knew that he was poor and that he was just deceiving me, but I was just doing labour without being paid. This moment, I thought in mind that it was quite sure that I would not be free from my inherited poverty.

After a while, I left his shrine as he was still attending to many people. With sadness, I went back to my room, I cast down and continued to think about my chronic poverty. I was still in sadness of being disappointed to get money in all my efforts when his youngest wife entered my room and she met me as I cast down sadly. She immediately asked from me: "What is wrong with you? Are you hungry?" I replied: "Not at all. I am not hungry. But I am thinking of my poverty and of my being disappointed to get money." She asked again: "Has the old man (Devil-doctor) not paid you since when you have been serving him?" I replied at the same time that: "He has not paid me even half a penny since when I have been serving him!"

When she heard so from me she grew annoyed. She kept quiet for a while and then she sat by my side very closely. Then she began to tell me: "You see, your master (Devil-doctor) is just deceiving you. He has no money which he can pay for you every month. You can serve him for even ten years but he will not pay you any money because he is poor. But now I shall be frank to you today that I like you to be my husband, and I am ready to follow you to your village anytime from now." But when she told me like that I thought in my mind at the same time that what I was thinking in my mind was far different from what this woman told me now. But after she had hesitated for a while to hear from me whether I agreed to what she told me but she did not hear anything from me. She asked with a lower voice: "Do you agree to what I have told you?" But I reluctantly said: "Yes, I have agreed to take you to my village and be my wife." I told her like that just to please her but I hated to take another man's wife.

Having heard from me that I agreed to take her to my village she was so happy that she stood up and danced for some minutes. After, she walked out, and after a few minutes I was surprised to see that she brought a very nice food for me. It was this day this youngest wife had started to treat me better than before and she was paying me frequent visit. But I was still serving her husband, the Devil-doctor, everyday. And I was still following him to the bush or forest or jungle to help him to carry almost all kinds of herbs with which he was preparing medicines because he was seriously banned to carry any kind of loads either by head or shoulders by the evil spirit which he was worshipping. Although he was poor but he was quite sure that one day his evil spirit would carry his good luck to his shrine for him. But he was strictly banned to carry loads by himself otherwise he would die as soon as the loads had touched his head.

For his poorness, his youngest wife was quarrelling with him always and she was telling him that she would divorce him if he did not find any other kind of the job to do which would fetch him sufficient money always. But of course whenever his wife advised him like that, he was telling her that his evil spirit had promised him that he (evil spirit) would carry good fortunes from the grove of the evil spirits to his shrine for him one day. So he was waiting for the good fortunes. This Devil-doctor was telling his youngest wife like that each time she quarrelled with him about money.

But this youngest wife was giving nice food to me regularly and she was telling me always to escape with her to my village as soon as possible. Although she was pressing me to do so but I could not leave this Devil-doctor as soon as his wife wanted me to do. Because I was afraid to leave him without his wish whenever I remembered that he had told me that if I failed to satisfy him, he would call the evil spirit which was in the lump of the iron back into it, he would tell me to carry it and he would then drive me away from his house even from that town. Now as the fear of this talking lump of the iron did not let me leave him for another town or my village. I continued to serve him without paying me any money. Thus I served him for five years and eleven months.

But in the twelfth month of the sixth year, one morning, at nine o'clock sharp, this Devil-doctor went to the grove of the evil spirits to bring a certain leaf for the special medicine which he wanted to prepare for one of his friends. This grove was about six miles away from the town. It was very big and was the home of all kinds of the evil spirits. He did not allow me to go there with him because I was not brave enough to see the evil spirits without being feared them. And if one feared them they would harm him or turn him to another thing. There was no any one of the other people of this town who was bold enough to enter this grove of the evil spirits except this Devil-doctor. In it, there were uncountable of the mighty trees, hills, rocks, etc., in which these evil spirits lived. There were uncountable of the paths on which they travelled from one place to another.

As soon as the Devil-doctor travelled to this grove that morning and entered it. He was going from one tree to another as quickly as he could and he was looking for the leaf that which he wanted to cut. He was doing so without seeing the right kind of the leaf that which he wanted to cut until he reached the heart of this grove. As he was still going along, he came to one mighty tree. At the foot of this tree he saw one very big pot. Its length was about four feet and the diameter was about three feet. It was full of pure corals which could be sold for more than four thousand pounds. This Devil-doctor did not believe his eyes when he saw this pot of corals. He stood before it and wiped both eyes with palm first for more than five minutes. When he became normal, with great surprise and happiness, he bent down, he examined some of them. Then he put them back in the pot, he stood up and began to think whether to carry this pot to his house.

As he was still wondering whether he was dreaming, he did not know when the happiness forced him to shout greatly: "Hah! I have got my good luck this morning! But how can I carry this pot of corals to my house now?" As soon as he shouted like that, he bent down, he lifted up the pot with all of his power. But as he was about to put it on head, it came to his mind this moment that he was not allowed to put any load on head by his evil spirit otherwise he would die as soon as it had touched his head. When he remembered that he was banned to put loads on head by his evil spirit, he hastily put the pot down on its place. Then he lifted his head up to the sky, he thought in mind that: "I am poor. I have no money and this (he pointed finger to the pot) is the pot of corals. The pot of wealth. If I can carry it to my house and sell them (corals) I shall become a wealthy man today! But I must not put any load on my head. But of course, my evil spirit who has warned me not to put any load on my head, had promised me that he would carry my good fortunes to my shrine by himself. Therefore, there is no need to worry myself to carry it to my house then. I am quite sure, my evil spirit will fulfil his promise today! Hah, I thank thee, my evil spirit!"

As soon as this poor Devil-doctor said like that within himself, he then left the pot there and returned to his house with the leaf which he cut.

When he entered his shrine, he sat on his usual chair with happiness. As soon he sat, he put the leaf down on the floor closely to his right hand. Then he told me to go and call his youngest wife for him. As soon as I left, he started to drink. When I came back with his wife he told her with smiling face to sit down before him. But before he started to tell her the story of the pot of the corals, he first told me to go to my room and I went out at the same time.

Then with smile, he told her the story of the pot of the corals: "You see, I have seen my wealth today when I went to the grove of the evil spirits to cut this leaf!" (he held the leaf up and showed it to her).

"Wealth? But I do not understand what you mean about that?" she was confused.

"I say when I went to the grove of the evil spirits this morning, I found one pot of corals! You know, the corals worth more than four thousand pounds!" he explained with smiling face.

"But where is the pot of corals now?" his wife shouted greatly.

"It is still at the foot of the tree where I have found it! It is there now!" he explained to her as he threw some drink into the mouth.

"Hah, you have left the pot of the corals where you have found it! I am sure, you will die in poverty! But of course, I have told you several times that I am going to divorce you soon! Yay! you have found the pot of the corals and you have not carried it to your house to be sold but you have brought one leaf instead! I shall repeat it, you will certainly die in poverty!" she sprang up, she slapped him on the back with both her palms as she was shouting loudly.

"Heh, just hold on and let me explain to you now! You see, my evil spirit had warned me not to carry any load with my head and he had promised me that he is the one who is going to carry my good luck to my house by himself. He had told me that I would certainly die if I let any load touch my head! And I am sure he will carry this pot of corals to my house soon!" the Devil doctor explained to his wife but all of his explanations were in vain. She did not believe him at all. Instead, she stood up and began to abuse him loudly as she was leaving the shrine.

As she had left the shrine, she did not branch to other

place but she came into my room direct. She sat on the same stool with me. Then I asked from her:

"What has happened to you?"

"You see, your master (the Devil-doctor) has found one pot of the corals at the foot of a tree in the grove of the evil spirits and he did not bring it to the house to be sold but he brought a single ordinary leaf instead!" She told me what her husband had found in the grove.

"He has found a pot containing corals and he did not bring it to the house!" I asked again as I held my head with a great zeal.

"Don't mind the hopeless Devil-doctor. He did not bring it to the house. But he told me that his evil spirit would carry it to the house for him!" she shouted as she was nearly crazy.

"Why has he left such a great wealth (corals) for the evil spirit to bring it to the house for him but not by himself? Why? Perhaps he was just telling you lie, because I cannot believe him any more!" I told her with a doubtful mind.

"Not at all. He did not tell me a lie. He is not a liar!" she confirmed all what he had told her about the corals.

"But he had promised me that he would be paying me some money every month the day I came to him but he has not paid me any money since that time! But of course 'a born and die baby makes the doctor a liar'. He is a liar in that respect or for failing to fulfil his promise!" I reminded her about the promise which the Devil-doctor had made but had failed to fulfil.

"Although he has failed to keep his promise, but I do not doubt the truth of the pot of the corals which he said that he has found at the foot of a mighty tree in the grove of the evil spirits. Because many wonderful things had been found in it by many brave people of this town, although it is dangerous to enter it. However, my advice now is that at nine o'clock tomorrow morning you will go to that grove of the evil spirits. Without fearing the evil spirits which are living there, you will be going from one mighty tree to another. I believe, after a few minutes you will see the pot of the corals. But do not waste time to carry it out of that grove. When you have carried it out, then you will hide it (pot of the corals) by side of the road on which to travel to your village. Having done so, then you will come back to the house and both of us will then escape with the pot of the corals to your village in the following morning. I believe, if we can carry the pot to your village and sell all of the corals, we shall become rich, so you will be free from your inherited poverty which has already become a chronic one!" This youngest wife of the Devil-doctor wanted both of us to carry the pot of the corals away to my village for she wanted her to be my wife at all costs.

As soon as she had advised me like that and I promised that I would follow her advice, she stood up and walked out of my room so that the families of the Devil-doctor or himself might not suspect our secret plans. After she had left, I dropped my head, I began to think about these plans again. Although I agreed to go to the grove of the evil spirits and carry the pot of the corals out of it and to escape with it from there to my village. But I did not like to escape with this youngest wife at all. After a while it came to my mind to carry the pot from that grove direct to my village instead to come back to the town to tell her. It was like that I planned to disappoint her.

On the following morning, before nine o'clock, she brought a nice food to me in my room. She went back as soon as she had put it down. Then I ate it to my satisfaction. But I hardly finished with the nice food when she walked into the room with one of her big cover-clothes. Having coiled it round, she gave it to me to put it on the head for carrying the pot. Having done so she went away. And when it was about nine o'clock, I took my matchet and bag, I hid both with the coiled cover-cloth under my dress so that the Devil-doctor, his families and his friends might not suspect that I was leaving the town for some place. I took these two my belongings (matchet and bag) along with me with the hope to start to go from the grove to my village and not to come back to the town to tell this youngest wife to follow me to my village. It was like that I planned to disappoint her. My plan to disappoint her was not in respect of the corals but because I did not like to escape with another man's wife.

As soon as I came to where this grove of the evil spirits was, I entered it and I began to go from one mighty tree to another with suspicion of not being killed or harmed by the evil spirits. As I was going deeply in it as quickly as I could and I was looking at the foot of everyone of the mighty trees. It was so these evil spirits were shouting greatly on me with their various kinds of fearful voices. And it was not so long when their fearful shouts made me feared so much that I began to tremble from foot to head with fear. However, I still kept going along zigzag with fear until I came to the heart of the grove. After a while, I saw this pot of the corals at the foot of one mighty tree. It was very huge indeed.

Without hesitation, I went closely to it as the terrible shouts of the evil spirits were hearing all over the grove like thunder. With great wonder and fear, I bent down, I examined some of those which were on top. But when I saw that they were pure corals which cost more than four thousand pounds. I did not know when happiness forced me to shout greatly: "Hah! This is a great wealth! No doubt, I am free from my inherited poverty today!"

Having shouted like that I began to dance round this pot of the corals. When I danced round it for a few minutes with great laughter, I hurriedly put the coiled cover-cloth on my head. Then I bent down and with all my power I lifted up the pot and I put it on my head. It was so heavy that three strong men could not even lift it up from the ground but the happiness which was in me this moment gave me the strength of about ten men with which I lifted it on to my head. But to my fear as I was about to leave that spot with the hope to be carrying it from there to my village. I heard a horrible voice which came out from this pot suddenly. The voice began to warn me so loudly that the whole of the grove was shaking. And it was this moment the voices of the terrible birds, animals, and all kinds of the evil spirits were hearing everywhere in the grove.

But as soon as I began to hear that the thing which was warning me was inside the pot. I wanted to throw the pot down and then run away for my life. But to my fear, I could not throw it down and I could not lift it up from my head this time. Instead I was hearing the warning continuously:

"Oh, yes, you have put me on your head better you carry me to the shrine of the Devil-doctor now! Make haste! Walk on your leg, my poor friend!" But I stopped to throw it down and run away when I heard that I should carry him to the shrine of the Devil-doctor. But it became so heavy this time that my neck began to sink down. I tried all my possible best to throw it (pot) down and run away but all my efforts failed. And I began to tremble from foot to head for the sudden heaviness of this pot immediately the warnings had started to come out of it.

After a while, I pretended to be falling down, but another terrible warning came from the pot suddenly: "If you fall down, you fall on your death! If you throw me down, you throw your life down! But be carrying me along to the Devil-doctor's shrine now! Make haste! You are keeping me too long on your head!" As I heard like that suddenly from this pot, I obeyed and I kept going along zigzag in this grove of the evil spirits. But to my surprise, I hardly kept going when this pot became as light as a feather.

As I was still carrying it along, to my utmost fear, there I saw that thousands of the evil spirits with whips in their hands were hurriedly coming out from the mighty trees, from the ground, from the tops and precipices of the mountains and cliffs, etc. All rushed to me and surrounded me. Without hesitation, they began to sing, dance and clap and they were flogging me continuously. I was in a great predicament this moment so that I lost all my senses at the same time but I was just staggering about in the circle. After they had whipped me for a few minutes as they were singing loudly thus: "The thieve of the corals, dance the dance of the punishment and let us see!" And as they were dancing and clapping round me, I did not know when I began to cry bitterly as I was staggering here and there in the circle. As soon as I began to cry and beg them for pardon, they stopped to flog me but they stood still in form of a circle and then they began to laugh at me.

Having laughed and made a mockery of me for a few minutes then the whole of them collected into one place and without hesitation some of them began to push me along in the grove towards the road of the Devil-doctor's town as the rest were shouting greatly—"The thieve of the corals," and were following me. Thus they were pushing me along until I came to the road. But as soon as they had pushed me to the road, the whole of them went back to their grove and were disappeared at the same time. Now I was alone on the road and I was carrying this pot of the corals along on it. Although I was confused whether the corals had turned to the evil spirit as soon as I had put the pot on my head. But after I had travelled far away from the grove, I turned my back to the Devil-doctor's town. To my fear again, I hardly started to go ahead with the hope to carry it to my village direct when the pot became so heavy suddenly and my neck then sank down into my chest for its heaviness. And within one second that it had become heavy like that, I heard the usual warnings which came out of it that: "Better you turn your face to the Devil-doctor's town now and carry me to his shrine!"

However, as I could not lift up my feet to go forward, willing or not, I turned my face to the Devil-doctor's town and I continued to carry this pot to his shrine. But to my surprise was that as soon as I continued to carry it along to his town, the pot then became as light as a feather. Now I was sure that there was no alternative unless I carried the pot to the shrine of the Devil-doctor. And as I was carrying it along on the road, it was so I was blaming myself that: "I was so stupid to believe the youngest wife of the Devil-doctor who had told me to go and carry pot of the corals from the grove of the evil spirits. Although when I saw the pot it was full of pure corals but these corals have now turned to an evil spirit. This means the youngest wife had deceived me so that I might be killed by the evil spirits. I am sorry, she has now put me in another punishment!" Not knowing that this youngest wife did not deceive me at all but it was myself who had wanted to take another man's (Devil-doctor) luck to my village.

However, I carried it to the shrine. But as soon as I entered the shrine, I heard another warning suddenly which came out of the pot: "Yes, you have carried me to the shrine! But put me down and then run out of this shrine at once otherwise you will lose your life! Put me down and run away!" So I hardly heard like that when I hastily put the pot down gently with fear and then I ran into my room which was in the other house, far away from there. But the Devil-doctor was not in the shrine when I carried it there, he was in his house together with his youngest wife.

When I entered my room, I sat down and dropped my head and then I began to think of the punishments which I received in respect of this pot of the corals.

After a while, the Devil-doctor went to his shrine but he was greatly wondered to meet this pot of the corals in his shrine. "Oh yes, this is the pot of the corals which I had seen at the foot of the mighty tree in the grove of the evil spirits when I went there yesterday! My evil spirit has brought the pot into my shrine as he had promised me that one day he would bring my good luck to my shrine by himself! I thank thee!" This Devil-doctor was so happy that he called his youngest wife loudly to come and see the wealth which his evil spirit had brought to him, for he did not know that I was the one who had brought it there although I was forced by the evil spirit which was in the pot to bring it there.

When the youngest wife came, he showed it to her, he threw the whole corals on the floor and as he began to examine them, he was telling her: "You see now! I had told you several times that my evil spirit would one day bring my good luck to me by himself! I told you yesterday that I saw one pot of the corals in the grove of the evil spirits but you grew annoyed that I did not bring it to the house! You see it here now! And I have become a wealthy man as from today!" When he showed this pot of the corals to his youngest wife with happiness. He began to look at her eyes whether she would be equally happy too. But instead, she scowled at him and then she left the shrine at once.

When she left the shrine she came to my room with the altercation. As I heard her altercation, I lifted my head up, I stood and with great anger, but she did not allow me to say anything when she shouted greatly with anger that: "You hopeless man who will really die in poverty! Our arrangement was to hide the pot of the corals on the side of the road and then to come back to me so that both of us might escape to your village with the pot of the corals! But why did you bring the pot to the shrine for the Devil-doctor? Oh, you have broken our covenant now. Hah, it is certain now that you will die in your inherited poverty! You hopeless man!" But she hardly said like that when I jumped up with anger as well and shouted on her: "But you are the one who is entirely hopeless! You are a cruel and merciless woman! If you are not so, you should have not told me to go and carry the pot from the grove of the evil spirits! Knowingly that evil spirit lives in it (pot) and that it will punish me! But you have just deceived me that the pot contained the corals! But you are the one who have broken our covenant! Go away, you are a deceiver!"

Having scolded her like that, she jumped up and slapped me on the face suddenly and I too slapped her on the face at the same time. Thus we continued to slap ourselves as she was blaming me loudly and I was blaming her loudly as well about this pot of the corals. Because both of us were confused. She thought that I wilfully carried the pot to the shrine instead to hide it somewhere on the road as she had told me to do. And I too thought that she had just deceived me to tell me that it were pure corals were in the pot. We were still slapping ourselves with great shout and exchange of words when the families of the Devil-doctor heard our angry shouts. They then rushed into my room but when they met us slapping each other, they parted us and asked us what had caused the fight.

She first explained to them that I had broken the covenant. They asked her to tell them the kind of the covenant which was between her and I. But of course when she did not tell them, I explained to them with earnestness that she told me to go and carry the pot of the corals from the grove of the evil spirits, but later on I found that it is the evil spirit that lives in the pot. But I hardly confessed to them when she explained to them as well that I was pressing her everyday that I wanted her to escape with me to my village and she denied that she had told me to go and carry the pot of the corals from the grove of the evil spirits.

But once the families of this Devil-doctor had heard from her when she shouted that "I had broken our covenant" they had understood that there was a secret plan between her and I and that she had agreed to escape with me to my village. So without hesitation, the whole of them pushed both of us roughly to the shrine. They hastily surrounded us as both of us stood before the Devil-doctor. When the families told the Devil-doctor that his wife and I had planned to escape to my village. He jumped up with great anger, he roared greatly like the thunder. After that, he asked from me: "You and my youngest wife have planned to escape to your village?" I hastily explained to him with fear that: "It is your wife who had told me to go and carry the pot of the corals from the grove of the evil spirits. But as soon as I had put the pot on my head the corals turned to an evil spirit!" When I explained to him briefly like that, he turned eyes to his wife and asked: "Is it true that you have told him to go and carry the pot from the grove?" But she denied. She explained that I had planned to escape to my village with the pot of the corals and herself.

Then as soon as she had explained to him like that, he bent down, he threw the corals on the floor and then told me that I did not carry any evil spirit to his shrine but the pure corals which he was going to sell for more than four thousand pounds. But to my surprise, when he threw these corals on the floor from the pot, I saw that in fact they were pure corals and not evil spirit as I had thought they were. Then he said loudly that if his wife had not agreed with me to escape to my village she should not have told me the secret of the corals. Then he with the help of his families pulled off the dresses of my body and then they wore my old dirty rags for me. After that they pushed me to the tree under which my lump of the iron was.

Then he bent down and began to incantate. Within a few minutes, the evil spirit of this lump of the iron came out from unknown place in form of a thick smoke and it entered the lump of the iron. To my fear, as soon as it had entered it back, this lump of the iron became alive. It started to make its usual terrible noises. Then without hesitation, he and his families put it on my head. And then they pushed me out of the shrine together with his wife. He told me that I should carry my burden which he had taken from me away from his town.

As I was carrying this talking terrible lump of the iron away from this town it was so I was cursing this youngest wife and it was so she too was cursing me loudly as she was going to her father's town. Thus both of us were driven away from this Devil-doctor's town with great shame. And it was like that I left this town with my poverty, with my usual burdens of the talking lump of the iron, with my usual dirty rags, with my old matchet and bag but without half a penny in hand.

Having travelled far away from the Devil-doctor's town, I put my talking lump of the iron down, I sat before it and then I began to think where to go again.

But when I did not know where to go again. Furthermore, I had now fed up to go to another town or village for money. Therefore, I put in mind to go back to my village which I had left several years ago in respect of my inherited poverty.

Having put my talking lump of the iron back on my head, I continued to travel along on the road. But with much difficulties, I came back to Ojo's and Alabi's village. When I came there, I asked for them with the hope to spend some days with them as the three of us were friends before. But I was greatly shocked when the people of their village told me that both of them had died a few weeks ago. They told me further that both died in the same midnight. When they told me so I remembered that six years ago, the Devil had shortened their lives from sixty-six to six years before he gave them uncountable bags of money in the midnight that they became his followers, but I refused to be his follower that midnight.

But I was not allowed to stay and rest for some days in this village when the people saw this talking lump of the iron on my head. However, I left there the same day. Thus I was carrying this lump of the iron to my village but with much difficulties. And within a few days that I had left Ojo's and Alabi's village, I reached my own village at about nine o'clock in the morning. As I was carrying it along in the village, and when the people saw me. They thought that I had become mad because of the dirty rags which I wore and also the talking lump of the iron which I carried instead to carry good thing. However, with great shame, I carried it to the house and I put it in one of the rooms.

217

After that I swept the whole house and compound as well. Having done so, I sat in my father's sitting room. After a while, many people came in to greet me for my safety return because many of them thought that I had been killed or died.

THE WITCH DOCTOR AND I IN MY
VILLAGE

∞∞∞∞∞∞∞∞∞∞∞∞∞∞∞∞∞∞∞∞∞∞∞

A tormentor forces his victims to be hardy.

*

Although I came back to my village safely but I came
back with my usual poverty which I had inherited
from my father and mother before they died. I came
back with dirty rags on my body, with my long sharp
matchet, with another burden which was the terrible
talking lump of the iron which the god of the Iron gave
me when Ojo, Alabi and I visited his town when the
three of us were returning from the town of the Creator.
But I came back without half a penny although Ojo
and Alabi were successful to get the money from Devil
but both of them had died after they had enjoyed the
money for only six years.

As the people of my village were coming to greet
me it was so some of them were bringing food and drinks
to me. I asked for my junior sister, AINA, from the
people but they told me that she and her husband had
left the village for the next one some years ago. Having heard so, I sent for her and she and her husband
came and greeted me. Having spent two days with me
they returned to their village.

But one day, when the people who came to greet me

were leaving for their houses, according to our custom, I led them to a short distance. I had forgotten that I must not be too far from the talking lump of the iron. To my fear and the people's, it shouted horribly and within a second it rolled heavily on the ground to the outside. As it began to warn me loudly that I must come back and put him on head before leading these people. Having seen this talking lump of the iron and as it was too fearful and strange to them. They fled away to their houses at the same time. So since this day the people of the village stopped to come to my house. But as I could not go and visit people without carrying it along with me, I stayed at home always. But I could not continue to do so for a long time because there was nothing for me to eat. Furthermore it did not allow me to go and work in the farm.

One morning, I sat down and began to think how I could be free from this talking lump of the iron for I was then nearly to die of hunger. After a while it came to my mind to carry it to Aina, my junior sister, in the next village, perhaps she and her husband would be able to feed me. Although I had the power to work for my living but this lump of the iron would not allow me to go out. Then in the following morning I put it on my head, I went to Aina and her husband with it. Luckily, I met both of them at home, they had not gone to the farm yet. As they saw me perspiring as if I had bathed they hastily helped me to put it down in one corner of their house. Having given me some minutes to rest, Aina gave me food.

But as I started to eat the food, she and her husband began to look at me with confusion. They were not sure whether or not I was mad. In fact, they were not to be blamed if they thought that I was mad because a person who was normal would never attempt to put such an ugly heavy lump of the iron as this on his head. But they did not know that it was not an ordinary lump of the iron. However, after I ate the food to my satisfaction, I told them what it was and also all the burdens which it was giving me. I told them further that the god of the Iron had given it to me to be worshipping it as my god.

Having told them the story of this talking lump of the iron, Aina's husband told me that he would take me to the great god of the Iron worshipper of that village. Without hesitation he and his wife, Aina, helped me to put it on my head. After that he took me to the great god of the Iron worshipper. He begged him to take it from me so that I might be free from the burdens that which it was giving me. Luckily, this great god of the Iron worshipper agreed to take it from me. But he told me to pay eight pounds to be spent for the sacrifice which he would make after the evil spirit of the lump of the iron had been driven back to the god of the Iron by his incantations.

But when he told me to pay eight pounds, I told him that I had no even half a penny in hand unless he would allow me to pawn myself to him for the money. I promised him that I would be working for him until when I would refund the eight pounds. He agreed when Aina's husband persuaded him but he told me that I should be working on his farm for one-third of the day everyday until I would pay him the eight pounds. When he said so I told him that I agreed to do so. Then on our presence, he sent for some dogs, cocks, etc. When all these things were brought, he incantated on this talking lump of the iron for many minutes before the thick smoke rushed out of it. As soon as the smoke disappeared he killed the dogs, etc. But the thick smoke was just like the figure of a human being, it was very ugly and its shape was not clear at all. It was like that I was free from this terrible talking lump of the iron although I pawned myself for money for my freedom.

Having thanked him greatly, we came back to the house and when I spent some days with Aina and her husband, I returned to my village. Now as I was free from the terrible talking lump of the iron, it was so I was free to go and work on the farm of the god of the Iron worshipper for one-third of the day everyday. And it was so I was free to go and work on my own farm for the rest two-third of the day for my leaving. Now I was happy although I was still in my poverty.

After some years, the people of the village advised me to find one lady to marry. I agreed but there was no money to pay for the dowry. Having explained to them like that they advised me again to pawn myself for money which was to be paid for the dowry. And I agreed to this advice as well. So after a few days, I went to another village, I contacted one wealthy pawnbroker who lived there. I pawned myself for the sum of twenty pounds. He told me that I should be working on his farm every-day for one-third of the day and I agreed. Now I had already pawned myself to two pawnbrokers for money and I was working on their farms everyday for two-thirds of the day and I was working on my own farm for the rest one-third of the day.

After a few weeks that I had got the twenty pounds, I found one beautiful and sensible lady. The twenty pounds was paid to her parents as her dowry and then she came to my house. Thus I married at last. But as I had already pawned myself to two pawnbrokers. I was working on the farm of the first one who had taken the talking iron from me, from seven o'clock to eleven o'clock in the morning. And I was working on the farm of the other who had given me the twenty pounds, from twelve o'clock to three o'clock in the afternoon. After that I was working on my own farm from four o'clock till the sunset. Thus I was doing everyday. Of course I had no sufficient food to eat although she was assisting me to do some work in the farm as she was not a lazy woman.

As I got no sufficient time to do plenty of work in my farm, within a few months, my poverty had become so much that we began to suffer for clothes, food, etc. But as everything was still growing from bad to worse everyday in respect of the insufficient time to work in my farm for our living. So having seen this, my wife advised me one day:

"Ajaiyi, better you go to the Witch Doctor of the village to find out from him the causes of this our fast growing poverty and to find out from him as well what can stop it!"

"But my poverty has been inherited from my father and mother before both of them died! And for this reason, I don't think there is no any witch doctor who can set me free from it! You see, I had been to the town of the Creator, the town of the god of Iron, the town of the fire creatures, the town under the river, the town of Devil-doctor, etc. in order to get money so that I might be free from the poverty. But at last, all my efforts were failed!" I explained to my wife like that with great sorrow.

"But of course you might have been to almost all the towns and villages in order to get money and you had failed in all of your efforts. You should not be discouraged at all. But you must be still struggling until when your poverty is conquered. Although you have inherited it but I want you to realize that everything is possible if one can endure the punishments of this world!" It was like this my wife convinced me to consult the Witch Doctor of my village about my poverty.

So at eight o'clock in the night, I went to the village Witch Doctor. I explained my difficulties to him with sorrow. But with a sharp and merciless voice the Witch Doctor replied:

"Yes, your case is quite simple. If you want to be free from your inherited poverty, you will buy nine rams and nine empty sacks. Having bought them and brought them to your house. You will put each of the rams alive inside of each of the nine empty sacks. Having done so, then in the midnight or when you are quite sure that the rest people in the village have slept. You will carry all to the grave of your father and put all on top of the grave. Having done so you must come and tell me that you have put them on top of the grave. But to be sure whether your dead father has taken the whole rams into his grave, you must go back to his grave in the following morning. And I am quite sure, you will meet only the empty sacks on top of the grave and that means your dead father has taken all the nine rams. But you should not forget to take that empty sacks back to your house and put them in your room and you will see that in a few days time, all will be filled up with money by your dead father and then you will be free from your poverty! But I shall remind you, you must come and tell me as soon as you have put the rams on top of the grave! Do not forget that!"

When the village Witch Doctor had explained to me what I should give to my dead father before I could be free from the poverty which I had inherited from him (father) before he died and he (Witch Doctor) warned me seriously that I must come and tell him as soon as I had put the rams on top of the grave. I stood up and thanked him before I left. But as I was returning to the house in the darkness, I started to think within myself:

"The Witch Doctor had said that unless I sacrifice nine rams to my dead father before he (father) would set me free from the poverty which I had inherited from him. But I believe, I will never free from this poverty because I have no money to buy even one cock how much more for nine rams and nine empty sacks." It was like that I was thinking in mind until I entered the house confusedly.

"What did the Witch Doctor tell you about your poverty, Ajaiyi?" my wife who was unable to sleep until I returned, hastily asked from me as I entered the house and I explained to her what he told me to do for my dead father. But when I told her that I had no money to buy the nine rams and nine empty sacks she said loudly: "Ah, you said you have no money to buy the nine rams and nine empty sacks! Are we going to die in this poverty or do you want your sons to inherit the poverty from you as well as you have inherited it from your own father? Better you go and pawn yourself to another

P   225

pawnbroker who will give you the money to buy the rams and the empty sacks!"

"Ah! To pawn myself to the third pawnbroker again! But I am afraid, if I do that again, it means I have pawned myself to three pawnbrokers. But how can I work for the three of them satisfactorily and who will be working for our living then?" I asked from my wife with sorrow.

"Never mind about our living, Ajaiyi. I believe, if you work hard, you will satisfy the three pawnbrokers!" my wife advised me strongly, and I agreed to go and pawn myself to the third pawnbroker who would give me the money to buy the nine rams and nine empty sacks.

In the following day, I went to the third pawnbroker who gave me ten pounds. Having given me the money he told me that I should be working on his farm for one-third of the day everyday and I agreed to do so. Now I would be working for the three pawnbrokers for the whole day and there would be no time for me to work on my own farm for our living any more.

However my wife and I went to the market with the ten pounds. But unfortunately, the ten pounds were not sufficient to buy the whole nine rams and nine empty sacks. Having seen this, I was so embarrassed that I told my wife to let us return to the house with the money.

"Oh, my husband, don't let us go home with this money without buying the rams and the empty sacks, otherwise we shall spend it for another thing and yet your poverty will still remain as worse as ever. But let us buy now as many rams and empty sacks as it can buy. Then in the midnight, you will carry them to the grave of your father. Having put them on top of the grave, you will then explain to the grave that you will bring the rest rams as soon as you have money to buy them. And I believe, your dead father will not refuse to accept them because he knew that he had left you in great poverty before he died!" Without argument I agreed when my wife advised me like that.

Then we bought six rams and six empty sacks that which the ten pounds could buy and we took them to the house. When it was midnight, I put each of the rams inside each of the empty sacks. All were alive when I put them in the sacks. Then I carried them one by one to the grave of my father which was half a mile to the village. Having put them on top of the grave, according to my wife's advice, I explained to the grave with a sorrowful voice: "My father, please accept these six rams from me as the first instalment and I shall not fail to bring the rest three for you as soon as you help me to get money to buy them!"

When I had done so, I went direct to the Witch Doctor. I told him that I had carried six rams to the grave. Having heard so, he thanked me with great laughter. After he had advised me strongly that I must not keep long before taking the rest three to the grave, and he chatted with me for some minutes, I came back to the house. But not knowing that I hardly left when this Witch Doctor and his servants went to the grave. They carried the whole six rams to his house and killed them for his food and without hesitation he gave the six empty sacks to one of his servants to return them to the grave before daybreak.

Hardly in the morning when my wife and I ran earnestly to the grave and both of us were very happy when

227

we met only the six empty sacks on top of the grave.
Without hesitation, we collected them and then returned
to the house with gladness. I hastily put them in one of
the rooms and then my wife and I were expecting that
all would soon be filled up with money. But having
waited and waited and waited for months but my dead
father did not fill these empty sacks with the money as
the Witch Doctor had told me. And this time my poverty
had become extremely worse and again the three pawnbrokers were dragging me here and there because I
could not work satisfactorily for each of them. I blamed
my wife with sorrow:

"I told you in the market that day that we should
return to the house with the ten pounds as it was not sufficient to buy the whole nine rams and nine empty sacks at a
time!"

"Ajaiyi, don't let us give up yet. We must try hard.
But my advice now is to go back to the Witch Doctor
and find out again why your poverty is still getting
worse even than ever before we had taken six rams to
your dead father and you should find out from him as
well why the six empty sacks have not been filled with
money by your father since when you have put them in
the room," my wife advised me gently like that.

Again, in the night, I went back to the Witch Doctor
and I asked him for the reason why my poverty was still
getting worse even than before the six rams were taken
to the grave of my father. I also told him that since
I had brought the empty sacks back to the house, they
had not yet been filled up with the money by my dead
father.

"Ah! Ajaiyi, your poverty cannot be stopped yet

and your dead father cannot fill the empty sacks with the money yet but when you take the rest three rams to his grave!" this Witch Doctor frightened me so much that I ran back to the house with great sorrow. And I told my wife what the Witch Doctor had told me to do before the empty sacks would be filled with the money by my dead father.

"What are we going to do next to get the money to buy the rest three rams and the empty sacks?" my wife asked calmly.

"As you know that we have no even one penny in hand, how much more to get such a big money to buy the three rams and sacks! But of course, what I am thinking in mind now to do is that when it is midnight. I will visit my father in his grave. I will ask from him that—'My father, you knew that I am in poverty before you died. But after you have died and buried, you are demanding nine rams from me but failing to give them to you, I will remain in poverty throughout my life time. Of course, I had tried all my best and brought six for you. Yet I was told by the same Witch Doctor that unless I bring the rest three on top of your grave before you would set me free from the poverty in which you had left me before you died!' " And I explained further to my wife that if my dead father confirmed all what the Witch Doctor had told me to do then I would behead him (my dead father) before I would come out of his grave.

"Ah, Ajaiyi, how can you manage to see your dead father? Please don't attempt to visit the dead," my wife feared greatly.

In the midnight, I sharpened my long and heavy

matchet which I had brought from my journeys. After that I took three of the six empty sacks which I put in the room with the hope that my dead father would fill them with the money. Then I went to the grave of my father. Having reached there, I filled two of the three sacks with the earth in such a perfect way that each seemed it contained a big ram. Having done so I put both on top of the grave. After that I left the third empty sack and my matchet behind the grave. Then I went to the Witch Doctor, I told him that I had put the rest three rams on top of the grave. He bursted into a great laughter when he heard so and he was still laughing loudly when I left him and I went back to the grave. As soon as I came back, I put the third empty sack on top of the grave as well. I held my matchet and then I entered inside it and cast down in it. Then I was waiting for my father to take these three sacks into his grave.

To my surprise when it was about two hours, the Witch Doctor and his servants walked in the darkness to the grave. He told his servants to carry these three sacks to his house. And the servants hardly put the sacks down before his gods when he began to loose them one by one with the hope to bring the rams out and then to return the empty sacks to the grave before daybreak as he did the first time that I put six rams on top of the grave.

But he was greatly shocked when he saw the earth in the first two sacks instead of rams and he hardly loosened the third when I jumped out of that one suddenly with my long and sharp matchet in hand, raised above head. Now as "a tormentor forces his victims to be hardy", it was so for this Witch Doctor this midnight:

"Hah! Ajaiyi, you were in the sack as well!" the Witch Doctor and his servants shouted dreadfully as they hastily defended their heads and faces with their palms.

Without hesitation, I walked wildly to the Witch Doctor. I stood firmly in front of him and his servants as I raised my long sharp matchet above head and then as I stared at him, I asked quietly: "Hun-un! So you have taken my rams for yourself and not my dead father! The rams in respect of which I have pawned myself to the third pawnbroker before I got the ten pounds with which I bought them! No doubt, you are finished this midnight! And . . ." this moment, as I was shouting greatly on him, the great anger began to shake me from foot to head.

"Oh, Ajaiyi, keep cool and let me confess to you now. It was not your dead father who had taken all your rams but I was the right person who had taken them and I had killed them for my food! I beg you now to forgive me!" the Witch Doctor, as the fear forced the perspiration to be rushing out of his body, he hastily confessed to me as I was preparing to matchet him and his servants to death.

"But I believe, you are my dead father who had taken my rams on top of the grave! Therefore, you are to set me free from my chronic poverty this midnight!" I shouted greatly on him as the great anger forced me to start to threaten him with the matchet.

"Not at all! I am not your dead father in any way but I am the Witch Doctor of this village! Therefore, I have no power to set you free from your poverty, and . . ." the Witch Doctor explained loudly with fear as he was trembling. But I hardly heard like that from him when I ran against him and snatched his right hand and then I asked loudly: "Tell me the truth now! Will you set me free from my inherited poverty this midnight?"

"Not at all! Only your dead father has the power to set you free from your pov. . . !" But as he was still explaining to me with a trembling voice. His servants rushed against me and he too hastily joined them. All of them held me and were trying to take the matchet from me. Having struggled hardly for a few minutes, the great anger gave me so much power this moment that I over-powered them when I struck some of them with the matchet. And without hesitation, I snatched the right hand of the Witch Doctor again and without mercy I began to drag him here and there in his sitting room.

But when he started to shout for help, I hastily closed up his mouth with the flat part of my matchet. Having seen this my dreadful action, all of his servants stretched up their hands, the great fear kept them quiet and then they hastily escaped to the outside.

"Certainly, you are my dead father who had taken all my rams and who will set me free from my poverty this midnight! Will you?" I roared greatly on him as I had then become as wild as a hungry lion.

"Ajaiyi, I am not a dead man! But I am the Witch Doctor of this village!" he murmured as his heart was throbbing with fear especially when he looked around and saw that all of his servants had been escaped to the outside for their lives.

"If you are a dead man or not, I don't mind! But show me where you keep all your money! Otherwise you are finished this midnight!" I shouted on him as I started to push him about with the pointed end of my matchet.

"Heh! Ajaiyi, don't kill me! Please follow me now to where I keep my money! Please don't kill me! But have mercy on me!"

Willing or not, the Witch Doctor walked with trembling body to the spot that he kept his money in a big pot which was half buried in front of his gods. Then with great fear of not being matcheted to death, he pointed finger to the big pot in which he kept all his money, which he had got from various people by his satanic way. So without hesitation, I pulled the pot out of the ground. I put it on my head and then I carried it to my house that midnight.

As soon as I had carried it to the house, I threw the whole money on the floor from the pot. But when my wife and I counted all, it was more than six thousand pounds. So it was this terrible midnight it was just revealed to me that it was this Witch Doctor who had taken my rams but not my dead father.

Although I had six thousand pounds from this Witch Doctor of my village with bravery, which he had got from the various people by his satanic way. Of course this money could free me from my poverty. But I did not spend it at all because it came to my mind this midnight that "money was father of sins and insincerities." And I remembered this midnight as well that Ojo, Alabi and I had been seriously warned in the town of the Creator that we should keep ourselves away from sins when we returned to our village. Furthermore, when the Head of the drummers of the Creator took us to the place of the punishments in the town of the Creator. I saw uncountable of the lords, millionaires, barristers, money-lenders, judges, etc. etc., who were in the greatest fire in respect of the sins which they had committed in order to get money before they died. So having remembered all this, instead to pay my debts out of this money, I simply kept it in the room.

But the following month, it came to my mind one night to build churches with this money. So I built one big church in my village, one in the village of the first pawnbroker who had taken the terrible talking heavy lump of the iron from me, one in the second pawnbroker who had given me the twenty pounds with which I had married my wife and one in the village of the third pawnbroker who had given me the ten pounds with which I bought the six rams and six empty sacks, with this six thousand pounds. After the four churches had been completed, with few people I started to worship the God Almighty in them every Sunday. I was then teaching the people the little I had learned about God from the town of the Creator. Within a few weeks, thousands of people from various villages and towns came and joined us when they heard that many people were healed from their sicknesses in one day by the prayers. All the evil worshippers, idol worshippers, etc. threw all their idols, etc. away and they joined us. Later on, this Witch Doctor too threw away all his gods and he joined us and it was not so long when he became one of the leaders. After some months, all the members of the churches, having understood that the God Almighty was the only to be worshipped and having seen that their prayers were heard by God, without asking them to help me with money. Each of them started to help me with a little money as he or she could. So within a few months I had plenty of money. Out of the money, I paid all of my debts and then I was free from my inherited poverty. It was like that I was entirely free from my inherited poverty at last but in a clean way.